A Donation has been made to the
Clay County Public Library
In Memory Of:

Claude McLerran

This Donation has been made by:

Roger & Pat Roberts

The SHOOTIN' SHERIFF

**Center Point
Large Print**

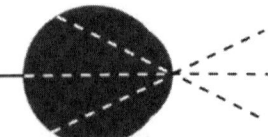

This Large Print Book carries the
Seal of Approval of N.A.V.H.

The SHOOTIN' SHERIFF

Nelson Nye

CENTER POINT PUBLISHING
THORNDIKE, MAINE

This Center Point Large Print edition
is published in the year 2011 by arrangement with
Golden West Literary Agency.

Copyright © 1938 by Nelson C. Nye.
Copyright © 1939 by Nelson C. Nye
in the British Commonwealth.
Copyright © renewed 1966 by Nelson C. Nye.

All rights reserved.

The text of this Large Print edition is unabridged.
In other aspects, this book may vary
from the original edition.
Printed in the United States of America
on permanent paper.
Set in 16-point Times New Roman type.

ISBN: 978-1-61173-248-1

Library of Congress Cataloging-in-Publication Data

Nye, Nelson C. (Nelson Coral), 1907–
 The shootin' sheriff / Nelson Nye. — Center Point large print ed.
   p. cm.
 ISBN 978-1-61173-248-1 (library binding : alk. paper)
 1. Large type books. I. Title.
PS3527.Y33S46 2011
813'.52—dc22

2011030019

I / *WILD BILL DORNE*

Down upon this man-for-breakfast cow town of Spavined Nag, the Arizona sun hurled its brassy, smashing rays with a definite fury. This was the hottest, lowest-ebb hour of any day—a time when gentlemen and roughnecks alike took their respite from the heat in whatever spots of coolness might be found.

Dorne knew it was this hour; knew it and did not care. Indeed, the knowledge of this very fact was what had sent him trudging through this burning, hock-deep dust of the deserted main street. It was his firm belief that this would be the best hour of the entire twenty-four for the doing of the chore he had in hand.

So it was with a definite purpose that he now was heading through the stifling dust between these gaunt flanking rows of bleached frame buildings towards the combination saloon, dance hall and gambling hell upon whose flaring false front was painted a fading legend:

GOLDEN STACK
Pecos Borst, Prop.

And this purpose of Dorne's was not a thing born on the spur of the moment; it was the thing for which yesterday he had been elected by a scant majority to pack the Sheriff's star. It was more—a purpose of prime importance to those "solid" citizens residing in this wild, raw town; a thing they had cherished in their secret hearts for many months.

"Wild Bill" Dorne they called this newly-elected sheriff. Lean of hip he was, and long of leg; a tall young giant with a slender wiry body holding immense reserves of strength and topped by the broad, tapering shoulders of a born fighter. A man who was held to be something of an expert in the old and gentle art of "draw-and-shoot."

Redheads, as a rule, are florid, or light of skin. But Dorne's was deeply bronzed, though his flaming mane was the colour of the adobe banks of the Little Red River. The eyes beneath this brilliant scalp adornment were a cold, clear blue, level and disconcerting. They had been known to hold a twinkle upon occasion, but were more often to be seen fairly glittering with frost, or with that wanton blazing reflection of a fiery temper out of leash. Below Bill Dorne's eyes was set a long Roman nose which more than once had been compared to a vulture's beak—though not within his hearing. Beneath this highly prominent and much advertised proboscis, a pair of long wide lips gashed his face above a rugged chin which, more often than not, could be seen swung forward at a stubborn jut. His cheekbones, to complete the picture, were high and flat, and the cheeks themselves a bit tight-pinched from the same source that had etched those radiating wrinkles about his eye-corners—long hours of saddle slicking beneath a broiling sun.

He was dressed in a somewhat ostentatious manner, as befitted a man with a name like his. His black J. B. was a ten-gallon hat, and a black-and-red checked flannel shirt covered the long rippling muscles of his upper body. Scarred black batwing chaps encased his long legs, and fancy Hyer boots peeped from their flaring bottoms, from the heels of which protruded huge silver gut-hooks with Texas-star rowels and pear-shaped danglers which, in the words of Bill himself, "shore tinkled one lovely tune." A lavender neckerchief was knotted loosely about his neck, and his wrists were covered by five-inch leather cuffs set off with silver wire.

But Bill was no dandy; he dressed this way because it suited his fancy; the things he wore were built as much for use as for appearance. Their use, as any man with half an eye could tell at a glance, had been long and steady. And the thick greasy cartridge belt girdling his lean hips looked as much a part of him as anything he wore, and the hickory stock of the heavy pistol, protruding from his low-slung, halfbreed holster, was shiny from an excess of handling.

Wild Bill Dorne most men named him, though there had been some—long since planted—who had been thoughtless enough to call him a thing less complimentary. And Dorne was a man who believed in meeting his obligations, no matter what their nature. He placed great value on his reputation for keeping his word.

It was that word which had placed him yesterday in the Sheriff's Office. And to-day he was starting out to make it good.

He was nearing the Golden Stack now, and could see the line of weary cow ponies chesting the peeled aspen rail beneath the warped wooden awning that crossed the boardwalk above the main entrance to Borst's resort. He was nearing it at the steady rolling gait of a man in whom determination was a definite thing.

Pecos Borst, as Dorne well knew, was overlord of this outlaws' paradise which a special meeting of legislature had defined on the maps as Spavined Nag. Well aware, too, was Dorne that Borst was one *cultus* hombre—"crooked as a dawg's hind laig." Suave and cunning, Borst was; as cunning as they came, and so damned suave that "butter wouldn't melt in his mouth."

It had long been hinted, as Dorne had heard, that Borst was taking a goodly cut from the wholesale activities being carried on by a band of unusually well-informed rustlers. Indeed, there was one rumour rife that Borst was not only the brains of the gang, but actually rodded it and led it upon its exasperating midnight forays.

But be that as it may, Bill Dorne knew from

personal observation—as many another gent likewise knew—that Pecos Borst was the "dawg with the brass collar" in this man's town. All things, by the salty and hard-case gentry who made this town their hangout, were deferred to Pecos Borst, who passed upon them or vetoed them according to the measure of profit in them for himself.

It was a fine state of affairs, as the solid citizens had pointed out more than once. It was, in fact, such a state of affairs as made the packing of the Sheriff's star one job most terrifically undesirable. Especially as the former incumbent had survived his election but a scant two hours.

But Wild Bill Dorne was packing the Sheriff's star now. And that made things a little different. For Dorne was a man—as the saying went—who had killed his men and buried them, and was like to do it again.

Bill packed the star and he aimed to perform. And right now, as he had declared to himself, was as good a time as any.

He crossed the walk and shoved himself through the swinging batwing doors and placed his back against a wall. There he stayed until his eyes had accustomed themselves to the dim light of the indoors after the change from the blazing sun outside. While standing thus, Bill Dorne took note that there was no sound in here save the droning of the flies and the ticking of the fat clock above the back bar.

Another man might have judged from this that the place was deserted save for a sleepy bartender or two. But not Bill Dorne; he reacted properly to such an unreasonable state of stillness. He figured that there were plenty of people filling the shadowy corners of this long main room—people who were holding their breath for the explosion of leaping weapons.

His vision cleared abruptly and he saw that he was right. At least twenty people had been lolling here upon his entrance; they were still here, but they were no longer lolling. Now they sat straight and rigid in the chairs about the gambling layouts; stood grimly motionless where they bellied the ornate black bar.

A faint grin quirked Wild Bill Dorne's wide lips as he glanced about him. Many times had he entered this place in the rôle of boisterous customer. And he knew many of the gathered assembly by their first names. But none smiled back at him now. They were woodenly noncommittal while waiting to learn what was up. For Wild Bill was the Sheriff now, and that was right apt to make some difference in which side of the fence a man had ought to be on.

Dorne's glance swept the room in one full comprehending stab. Borst's tinhorns, lookouts and bouncers were in their accustomed places.

Lola, too, sat inscrutably behind her faro table, sheathed to-day in a pale blue gown that brought out the richness of her tall blonde beauty and made the most of her full lithe figure that seemed as if it had been poured into the thin fabric of that low-cut dress.

But there was a difference here, to-day. Dorne recognized at once that Borst was ready for him. His flashing glance had noted where the hands of Borst's men hung. And he had noted, too, how men were unostentatiously slipping away from close proximity to himself and to Pecos Borst, where he stood with thumbs hooked into the armholes of his elaborately embroidered vest.

Bill's grin tightened a bit, but it stayed right there on his lips.

Pecos Borst was smiling, too; suavely, smoothly, dangerously. He rolled the fat cigar across his thick mouth and chuckled deep down in his great bull throat.

"Howdy, Bill. How's it feel to be the Sheriff of this man's town?"

"Can't tell yet," Dorne said. "Ain't been in office long enough. Guess you know what I'm here for, Pecos."

Borst drawled, "Sure. An' thanks, Bill. You came over here to spread the good news that you've got everything fixed, an' that the Golden Stack can go right on like usual."

Dorne's easy laugh mocked the tightening

stillness. "Why, no, Pecos," he said. "I came over here to serve you warnin'. This town is plumb fed up with the way you've been runnin' things. You can shoot it out or you can hoof it out. But out you're goin'. The choice is up to you."

II / TWO GIRLS

Bill Dorne had long been known as a wild and reckless ranny to the folk of Spavined Nag. But it took an inordinate amount of gall to stand up here and tell Pecos Borst to his face that he had to get out of town. The whiteness of listening customers' faces and the rigidity of their bodies amply testified to this.

Borst's big rocklike figure did not shift its posture by so much as a twitching muscle. Nor did the expression change on his beefy, florid face. But his eyes showed suddenly smoky behind his sleepy lids.

"You surprise me, Bill," Borst said, and his head moved restlessly, throwing his long-eyed glance around the room. This sizing-up of the crowd was a constant thing with him. A habit it was, and unbreakable. For it rose from long-grounded instincts of self-preservation. "In fact, Bill, you disappoint me. I figured you for more sense than that."

"You're a cool one," Dorne commented, laying his regard upon Borst closely. "But cool or hot, you're goin' out. Them's orders, an' you better make up yore mind to seein' they're carried out."

Borst's voice was soft as the purring of a cat: "Are you allowin' you're man enough to give me orders, Bill?"

"We won't be goin' into that. You've got yore choice. See that you take it before sundown. Because after that you won't have a choice any longer," Bill Dorne concluded, and a wide grin fired up his face.

Ignoring Borst then, Dorne tilted his hat to a rakish angle and moved off towards the girl at the faro layout. It was like a slap in the face to Borst. But the overlord of Spavined Nag turned away, on his beefy face a look that was reserved and thoughtful. Whatever move he had in mind, one thing was certain: it would get no advertising in advance. For he was like that—sudden.

Bill Dorne stopped before the faro table. It was deserted now, save for the lithe blonde goddess who sat behind it. Her eyes were on his gravely, inscrutably. No one had ever known Lola's face to betray the secrets of her head. Or heart. She kept things to herself, exhibiting to the world a cold smooth face whose pallor and poker calm could not be pierced. And, though her figure was like a living flame, and as easily seen, men treated her with respect. For Lola had been around and knew a thing or two about keeping gents in their places.

In her eyes and poise, in her impenetrable calm—the very atmosphere about her, Bill had always found a quality hard to define. Accurate description would have labelled her exotic. But she was more than that; in Bill she awoke an eagerness, a pulsing excitement, he could not understand.

As she returned his steady glance, her red lips made a long and wistful curve against the alabaster pallor of her face. And slowly, under his close regard, her cheeks took on a tint of rose.

Bill saw this change and was flattered by it. But he would have been hard put to give the reason for his feeling. He could, however, have offered many reasons as to why he should give this woman a wide berth. He didn't, though; not even to himself.

He felt again that sense of wild elation which she always stirred in him. Perhaps it was because unconsciously he sensed in her a kindred nature, an equal love of wild abandon—a deeper, fuller hunger for the fierce emotions of a dangerous living. Though God knows she never had given him cause to sense such things.

She kept herself to herself, and always had. So far as he knew. And she treated him no better than other men who had looked upon the wine when it was red, and had gambled away their money at the beckon of her rare smile. She treated them all alike and screened herself behind a cold hard barrier of aloof reserve. A reserve that hinted there were certain limits to the familiarity a man might attain. And that beyond those limits a man would travel at his own risk. And that it would be a risk was evidenced quite often by the wicked light that flashed far back in the jade-green depths of Lola's eyes when men tried to lay foundations for a more intimate relation. Those eyes of Lola's warned that she would feel no compunction about using that pearl-handled little derringer that always peeped from her bodice.

"How are you, Bill?" she said. "We haven't seen you for a full twelve hours."

"I been busy," he said, sighing. "This sheriffin' keeps me busier'n a dawg with fleas. 'F I'd 'a' knowed there was so danged much deskwork to runnin' this office I sure wouldn't 'a' let 'em put my name on that durned ticket. I got to get me some help befo' I bust a gut, or somethin'."

She gave him a little smile. One of the few he'd ever seen upon those ripe, red lips of hers. It transformed her instantly. Brightening her features. Adding fire and zest, and hazing a luring sparkle into the hard green of her eyes. Bill thought her teeth the whitest he had ever seen, and the most even. Then the smile was gone and the old inscrutable mask was back upon the alabaster whiteness of her cheeks.

"How's your engagement getting on?" she asked. "Got the date set yet?"

Embarrassment put a dull glow across Dorne's face. And her words brought conflicting emotions to the surfaces of his eyes; amazement, chagrin and anger.

"How'd you know about that engagement?" he growled softly.

She regarded him gravely, wistfully almost, one might have said. "Shucks, Bill. You're too important a figure in this community not to have all your comings and goings vigilanced. Shucks, I'm betting they knew it here five minutes after you'd popped the question. Last night it was, wasn't it? Right after you'd been elected?"

Bill swore, and then apologized. "It's sure got me fightin' my hat," he growled, "how Borst gets onto things so quick. It sure is amazin'. I reckon you know—"

"Who she is? Of course. Marcia Globe, the Mayor's daughter. You've got a keen eye, Bill. I congratulate you."

He took her small pale hand in his big brown one, and held her fingers as though they had been eggs. He was wondering if he had detected a catch in her voice, or if he had just imagined it. Desire, he thought irrelevantly, sure is the pappy to a peck of things.

"Well that's right nice of you, Lola," he said. "I don't know anyone whose congratulations I'd rather have."

He became conscious abruptly—as she sought to pull it loose—that he still held her hand. He released it with another flush. And had difficulty smothering an oath. Why was it, he wondered, that he blushed so dash-burned easy? It usually happened, he recalled, when he was around this Lola girl.

"Have you set the date yet?" she repeated, affecting a show of interest he was sure she did not feel.

"Why, no," he said. "I'm lettin' Marcia tend to that. Women like to do them little things, some fella told me once. I wouldn't wanta cut her out of any of the fuss an' fixin's."

But very seldom had Bill ever penetrated the poker veil of opaque green with which her eyes screened away her thoughts. But he read something into the expression of her eyes right now, a pure emotion—fear.

It spun him wickedly on his heels and sent his right hand slapping towards that pistol slung in the half-breed holster at his hip. The pistol's detonation and leaping burst of flame seemed identical with another. But it was the man across the room whose hands clutched frenziedly at his chest while he tottered there swaying, before he crumpled on his face.

Bill's gun weaved slowly back and forth. His eyes raked those faces turned to his with slashing contempt. Eyes shifted and slid away before that icy glance. "Anyone figurin' to take up where he left off?"

But under that pistol's steady stare and the reckless challenge in the smoky eyes of Dorne, no man moved. Several had got their hands above their heads, and they kept them there, fearfully. Dorne looked straight at Borst.

"You wantin' any?" he asked.

Borst slowly moved his head from side to side in a negative gesture. He did not look scared. Merely amused. For his heavy face showed a thin smiling.

Bill Dorne sneered, "Caution can sure be learned quick by the misfortunes of others."

Borst chuckled deep down in his throat as though amused by some secret thought. Then abruptly he quit smiling; the change threw a shadowed light across the brightness of his eyes.

"One of these days, Billy boy, you're goin' to go too far. When that day comes—"

Malicious desire spread a reckless look across Bill Dorne's cheeks. "When that day comes, you ain' goin' to be around, Borst. Not unless you make yore play right now."

Borst's craglike, beefy face did not change expression. "I'll even that score in my own good time," he said, and lit a new cigar.

"Yore time," Bill reminded grimly, "is gettin' mighty short."

But Borst just grinned. "I'm the best judge of that, Bill," he answered, and turned away, catching the eye of the white-faced piano player. "All right, Professor. Strike up a tune."

Bill left the Golden Stack and, crossing the dusty street, chimed his spurs down the opposite side. When he came before a white frame house trimmed with green, he turned in the gate. A couple of steps later he was mounting the wooden steps to the veranda. This was the home of Mayor Globe, one of the only two buildings in town to be garnished by a coat of paint (the other building was the church). It was on the outskirts of the town.

As Dorne stepped upon the veranda, the door opened and in it stood framed a girl of rare loveliness. Her oval face was softly tanned and there was a natural colour in her cheeks. Her eyes, of a soft clear brown, were topaz bright behind her curling lashes. They were smiling, level eyes—eyes which always filled Bill Dorne with a new calm and smoothed the turbulence from him like a wand of Peace. They did it now.

"Bill!" she said, and he thought it lucky guns were fired so often in this town that she did not think to ask him for an explanation of the shot she must have heard a few minutes back. "I'm glad you came. It's so lonely here when Dad's uptown. Stay awhile, won't you?" And, at his nod, "Come on inside; it's cooler there."

He could not help but admire her as he sat in a chair facing hers across the room. It did not seem possible, he told himself, that she could be engaged to him. Such luck was hard to realize.

She was dark, and her jet black hair held a soft blue sheen where light from the open window struck across it. She rose to her feet abruptly and came across to him. He stood up, wondering. And blushed like a schoolboy when she offered him her lips.

He kissed her awkwardly and somehow felt a little guilty. Why, it would be hard to say. No one ever would have thought of Marcia Globe as any goddess that a good strong kiss would sully. There was too much light and laughter to her.

They talked some while of this and that. And then Bill rose to go.

"Gotta be gettin' back to the grindstone," he muttered, self-consciously. "You mightn't think it, but there sure is a pile of deskwork connected with sheriffin' that I never woulda believed before I got this job. Kinda makes a fella wish he'd stuck with cows. I gotta good mind to call Dave Kierny, or one of the other boys in to help me."

"But Kierny's your foreman," Marcia protested. "Who'd run your ranch if—"

"Oh, I couldn't spare him from the outfit," Bill Dorne answered. "But I sure wisht I could. Wonder how a fella goes about gettin' a deputy? Reckon I could advertise for one? Like city folks do when they want a house?"

Marcia shook her head. "I don't think so. I can ask Dad. He'd know."

Dorne nodded. "Well, I'll be seein' you after a while."

"Yes, of course. You'll come to supper, won't you?"

"I ain't right sure that I'll be able," Bill said,

flushing again. "But I'll sure come if I can find a chance."

Leaving the Mayor's house, Dorne started back up town. On his way he got to thinking over that business in the Golden Stack. He would, he reflected grimly, be willing to bet his first month's pay as Sheriff that Borst had put that tinhorn up to trying to pot him in the back. It had the mark of Borst's methods. For Borst believed in never doing himself anything he could get some other gent to do for him. Especially if there was apt to be any risk attached to it.

It was uncommon odd, he mused, that Borst's pet pair of gunslammers had not been around to scare up a little excitement when he'd called. Uncommon odd. For Borst hired Smoky Leupp and Joe Fuddabaugh solely for their proficiency with pistols. And Borst was not a man to pay out good money to gents who weren't around when they were needed.

As he came in sight of the Sheriff's Office, he slowed down his long-legged stride. A man was lounging near the door. An unsavoury looking customer. Shabbily dressed. And with one hand hooked into the greasy gun belt that sagged from a lanky hip.

III / A MAN WANTS ACTION

"Well, pilgrim," Dorne said. "What can I do for you?"

"What would yuh be expectin' tuh do?"

Dorne looked him over carefully. The fellow was dressed in a patched orange flannel shirt, over which he wore a greasy vest, and a pair of frazzled corduroy trousers stuffed into scuffed half-boots with run-down heels. These boots were equipped with tin-belly spurs whose rowels were missing. A faded blue scarf was pulled tight about his scrawny neck, and a floppy-brimmed sombrero was shoved far back on his shaggy head. His face was gaunt and wrinkled, and was covered by a three-days' stubble of beard.

Dorne said, "From the look of you I'd say you was lookin' for a night's lodging at the expense of the county."

The ragged stranger grinned widely. "Wal, yo're right in a way. I am—but not jest like yo're figgerin'. I'm lookin' for a job."

"Job?"

"Yeah. I hear yo're aimin' to curb the wickedness of this hell-roarin' town. Brother, yo're goin' to need some depities. Fact is, yo're lookin' at the first candidate right now."

"You think so?"

"I know it!"

"What qualities you got that make you think you'd be considered as a possibility?" Dorne asked sceptically. "You don't look so hot."

"Hot!" the stranger snorted. "This is the thirstiest country ever I hit! I'm hotter'n the hinges of hell—which goes to show appearances is some deceptive."

"I'm talkin' about qualifications for this deputy job you mentioned."

"Wal, Mister, yo're lookin' at the shootin'est ranny what ever come down the pike; a pistol-slapper on which yuh kin smell the powder smoke an' brimstone! Brother, if yuh don't take me on—"

"It won't do you any good to hand me any sob stories," Dorne cut in hastily. "I came from Missouri an—"

"Yuh did! Wal, I'll be a purple prairie dawg! So'd I! Shake, Missouri!" and the stranger stuck out a grimy paw.

But Bill Dorne looked it over suspiciously. "I ain't bitin' on that one," he grunted. "You wouldn't be the first gun man—if you *are* a gun man—to shoot down the gent whose hand you grabbed."

"Wal, prancin' prairie chickens! *If I am* a gun man says he!" and the stranger's right hand suddenly spouted flame and lead. And while the echoes of his shots slammed back and forth between the sun-bleached buildings, Dorne stared incredulously at the outline of himself which, with six leaden slugs, the ragged stranger had blasted against the adobe wall!

He smothered an admiring oath and said, "What handle do you go by?"

"Tranter's my name—Buck Tranter. Though there's some as calls me Brimstone."

"Well, Tranter, you're a pretty good shot."

"Pretty good!" Tranter snorted. "If you kin do better, an' in quicker time, I wanta know! Brother, that shootin' of mine's DAMN good! You can take it from a man what knows."

"You sure ain't shy on brag," Dorne chuckled. "But will you work?"

"Work! Why, Mister, I'm the hardest workin' cuss you'll meet up with in forty-eight states—bar none. I'm a genuwine early riser what don't bed down until the wee small hours, account I'm so dang scared that some 'un might say Buck Tranter ain't a-earnin' his keep!"

Dorne eyed him sceptically. "Don't look much like you been garnerin' the rewards of such steady an' ga'ntin' work."

"It's 'cause I ain't had any work for a calendar of Sundays," Tranter said, and bit himself off a chew from the plug of Brown's Mule which he took from his right hip pocket. "Honest work is sure scarcer round this country than hen's teeth. Never saw such a place. Arizony ain't what she used ter be. Why, I can remember the time when all a fella had ter do ter earn a livin' in this yere state, was ter swing a lass rope free an' easy, an' carry along a extra cinch ring in his saddle pocket. With a tolerable display of hawss sense an' a fair amount of labour a man could make quite a pocketful of change in a mighty few hours."

"Bein's you're puttin' in yore bid for a deputy's job, I take it you've reformed a bit since them days," Dorne suggested.

"Reformed?" Tranter scowled. "Hell, yes! I sh'd say I hev. I goes to church reglar now, ever' Sunday. Don't smoke, don't cuss, don't chew an' never slap m' brand on another man's steers. Brother, I've reformed so dang much it hurts!" Tranter's scowl grew fiercer. "Why, dang it, Mister, I've even took ter usin' soap an' water since I got the Word. I never thought I'd see the day when I'd lay my cheek ag'in' a chunk of soap! But there it is. I'm a reformed character, as they say in the book."

"I think I could use a gentleman of yore type," Bill grinned. "But there's one thing I gotta tell you first, Brimstone. This here's a tough town. I'm goin' to tame it if I have to bust a gut. Goin' to gentle 'er so she'll eat right outa my hand, so's to speak. But right now she's hotter than hell on wheels. Eats herself a man for breakfast every mornin' reg'lar. If you want the job, knowin' that, then she's yores."

"Brother, she is mine," said Tranter, and stuck

forth his grimy paw again. This time Bill took it, and was surprised at the strength in Tranter's hand.

"You've got a grip," began Bill.

But Tranter interrupted with a dismal smile. "Not bad. But yuh can't have one thing without yo're missin' someplace else. With me it's a strong back an' weak mind. But it really ain't my fault. I got dropped out of a prairie schooner along the River Pecos when m'folks was migratin' from Missouri. Saint Louis is where I hail from, Brother. Good ol' St. L! I was right tender at the time."

Looking at him, Dorne could hardly imagine a time when this lanky, grimy, wrinkled-faced specimen had ever been tender. But he just grinned. "Well, hang yore hat up in the Sheriff's Office—just inside the door here, Buck—an' get busy on that pile of papers you'll see on my desk. I'm goin' down the street a spell to wet my whistle."

Tranter stuck his head inside the door, took a look at the papers, and hurriedly pulled it out. "Say!" he wailed. "You don't expect me to mess around with no damn papers in this heat, do yuh?"

"That's what I'm hirin' you for."

"But I got a whistle, too," Tranter objected. "An' this godawful heat has done curled 'er up like a dry leaf."

"Little more curlin' won't hurt it, then," Bill decided, and started off.

Tranter swore disgustedly. "An' here I thought this was a hell-bendin' town plumb sufferin' from the lack of a two-fisted gun-slammin' depity which knows which end of the tube the smoke curls outen! Hell! There ain't no justice any more!"

Bill Dorne turned round, a cold gleam sparkling in his eye. "Do you want the job, or don'tcha?"

"Course I want the job—"

"Then quit gripin' an' stick up yore right paw while I swear you in."

Tranter did so and was sworn in without further waste of time. Bill got a deputy's badge from the desk drawer and handed it to him. Tranter looked it over admiringly, spat on it, and shined it up on his shirt tail. After which he pinned it on. Thrusting his arms akimbo, he stood considering it with a peculiar expression.

"First time," he said, "I ever wore one of them. I can picture a coupla gents which would spin round in their graves like a top, was they to see me now. Buck Tranter, Depity! Cripes! I feel plumb dolled up like a little red waggin."

In the combination saloon, gambling hell and dance hall behind the faded sign bearing the words GOLDEN STACK, Pecos Borst was in earnest conversation with a pair of his trusted smoke-and-lead experts. To wit, Messrs. Leupp and Fuddabaugh. His tone was lowered and what he said was evidently to the point, for leers of pleasant anticipation overspread his listeners' evil countenances.

They moved to the door. "An' be sure there ain't no slips," Borst sent purring words after them. "An' on yore way out, send in Phoenix John Muroc an' Mendota."

While he was waiting, Borst entered a few figures in the little black book he always carried in the left breast pocket of his coat. Then he peeled the cellophane from a fat cigar and, biting off an end, placed the weed between his lips and lit it. With spirals of pale blue smoke wafting ceilingward, he settled comfortably back in his padded chair.

Came a knock on the door.

"Come in."

Two men entered the room. The first, Phoenix John, was dressed in the dark funereal garments of a professional gambler. He wore a diamond in the starched front of his white shirt, and there were lacy ruffs extending beyond the black sleeves of his coat. And a string tie at his throat. A stovepipe hat sat jauntily upon his head, and the face below it was a sombre unsmiling mask.

Behind him appeared a Mexican breed, handsome despite the tight-pressed gash that served him for a mouth. Pedro Mendota's forbears—on his mother's side—had walked in moccasins. And it was plain, by the dark little eyes alive with flashing sparkles, that Pedro felt no shame for the fact. He was clad in a tight-fitting jacket of blue velvet, and wore Mexican chaps over his leg-clutching trousers of green corduroy. A high-peaked straw sombrero, a-glitter with thread of gold, was thonged to his head by a chinstrap that was looped through a silver concho. The cartridge belt circling his panther-lean hips sagged in the middle to the weight of the bone-handled Colt that filled its flapless, brass-studded holster.

"Mendota," Borst said softly, "how long'll it take you to round up the boys?"

Mendota rasped a smooth brown hand across his chin, then grinned in a way that displayed to advantage his flashing teeth. "Mebbeso three hours?"

"That'll do," Borst nodded. "Take 'em over to Globe's ranch to-night. Cut his fences all to hell an' run off every two-year-old you can get yore hands on. Savvy?"

"*Si, si!*" Mendota chuckled slyly. "Thees Jefe, he weel be the one mad hombre, *no*?"

"I'm gonna own every decent spread in this county before I get done," Borst said in a way that took the brag from his words. "You fellas string along with me, an' by Gawd, we'll show some folks a thing or two! I'm figurin' to go places, an' them that trails with me are a heap likely to get their pockets lined."

Phoenix John eyed him dourly, saying nothing. Mendota grinned.

"All right, Pete. Get started. We're hittin' Globe hard to-night. Globe is the one that put Dorne up for sheriff an'—"

"What about Dorne," interposed Phoenix John drily. "Ain't you sort of leavin' him out of your calculations?"

"I'm not leaving anything out—or anybody," Borst said. "I'll take care of Bill Dorne when it suits my book."

"Take the cattle to the usual place?"

Borst nodded. "An' don't be afraid to use yore guns if any of Globe's half-baked punchers try to interfere. But keep yore lead clear of Polsky. I ain't through with him yet."

Mendota nodded and left the room, dragging his spurs.

"Shut the door," Borst told the gambler, and when the door had been closed: "Sit down. I got a few things I wanta say to you."

Phoenix John was settling himself in his chair when Borst stepped on a buzzer. A moment later one of the bartenders stuck his head in the door. "Call Lola. I want her in here," Borst said, and the white-aproned man disappeared.

Borst turned his smoke-grey eyes on Phoenix John. "If Dorne, or any of his friends, play in here I want you to see that they get cleaned proper. But don't pull anything crude; I don't want Dorne makin' a sieve out of you. Understand?"

"Yeah."

"All right. Pass the word around. When you go out, send in Gleed."

Phoenix John stared at Borst for a long silent moment, then got carefully to his feet and left the room.

Gleed and Lola came in together. Borst scowled at the girl. "Took yore time, didn't you?"

"Were you in a hurry? Ed just said you wanted to see me when I got through. I was racking the chips for to-night's game—"

"Never mind the alibis. That ain't what I'm hirin' you for." Borst's smoky eyes fastened on her face with a close regard, with a probing, penetrating stare. "Dorne stops by to pass the time of day quite frequent with you, I been noticin'. You ain't pullin' no fast ones on me, are you?"

"What do you mean?"

"Like, mebbe, tellin' him to lay off my game. He ain't been playin' at all lately." His glance grew opaque and flintlike. "If I thought for one minute—"

He let his words trail off, but his cheeks were harsh with the unspoken threat.

Lola looked at him and laughed, a swift tinkle of mirth. "Don't be a fool," she said. "What do I care about Wild Bill Dorne?"

"That's what I'd like to know," Borst said, and turned to Gleed.

"Put everyone to work gettin' the stuff packed up. Send somebody down to the freight office an' have 'em get a coupla their biggest wagons up here right away. We're movin' out."

Gleed's pugnacious jaw fell open and he stared at his employer with a look of stunned surprise. Then his jaw swung shut with a heavy snap and he growled an incredulous oath. "By cripes, I allus knew Bill Dorne was plenty tough, but I'd never believe he was tough enough to put the Injun sign on you!"

"Save that wind to cool yore beans," Borst growled softly. "He ain't puttin' no Injun sign on nobody—me, least of all. I been contemplatin' this move for some while, an' this gives me the chance to put it through without no questions bein' asked. We're movin' to that ol' Seldies place three miles out. You know that ol' 'dobe?"

Gleed, Borst's head bouncer, nodded. "I know the place all right, but I'll be damned if I know what you're wantin' to shove way out there for! You may be doin' this for yer own good reasons, but this whole damn town's goin' to say we moved 'cause Dorne run us out. We'll never live it down—we'll be the laffin' stock of the whole blame country!"

Borst was a man who knew the value of a long silence; more than once he'd made silence worth its length in gold. He tried it on Gleed now, while he held the man with his smouldering, opaque eyes.

Gleed was a hard case; a bar-room bruiser who

was an expert in his line. A man with sledgelike fists and gorilla torso. Six-foot-four he was, and weighed around two-sixty. Cauliflower ears adorned a face that was huge and flat; a bullet-headed face with a broken nose and a jutting, pugnacious jaw. Yet under Borst's fixed regard he shifted uneasily.

Borst's voice, when at last he spoke, was smooth and cool: "You doin' the talkin' round here now?"

Gleed shook his bullet head hastily. "Not me, boss. I was on'y—"

"Then shut up," Borst said, and peeled three-four bills of large denomination from a roll he pulled out of his pocket. These bills he tossed across the table. "Get busy. I want this joint moved out of town before sundown. An' I want our new location ready to open up in time for the evenin' trade."

Gleed took the bills, stuffed them in his pants and went out, shutting the door softly back of him. When the door was thoroughly closed, Borst turned back to Lola.

"Well," he said, "that's that. We'll open up tonight in the old Seldies place. Dorne'll play hell runnin' us out of there."

Lola was looking at him thoughtfully. "It all depends . . . I wouldn't be too sure. Bill Dorne's got a mind of his own and he's a man who don't know the meaning of the word fear."

Borst scowled. "He'll know what fear is 'fore I

get done with him! Who the hell's Bill Dorne, that he can give me orders? He's crossed me more'n once. But he ain't crossin' me no more—not after we move outside the town—"

"Bill Dorne's the sheriff," Lola reminded him. "Town boundaries don't mean anything in his reckless life—nor county boundaries, neither."

Borst swore vividly. "That fella's huntin' a quick grave if he messes with me any more! I'm fed up! He'll keep his hooked beak outa my business from now on or he'll get himself rubbed out! We're goin' to run the Golden Stack wide open. Everything goes. An' another thing I've meant to *habla* to you about, sister—from here on out I wanta see the percentage of profits from yore game go up. Either they go up, or you find yourself a job some other place! I want some action—an' I'm goin' to get it!"

IV / TUMBLEWEED

When Dorne left his newly-hired deputy in the Sheriff's Office, with orders to clean up the neglected correspondence and other papers littering the sheriff's desk, he set out down the street at his easy, swinging stride with no definite purpose in his mind—unless the dodging of that detested deskwork could be so described.

Tranter, he had a hunch, was going to be a great comfort.

He found himself wondering, as he wandered aimlessly along, just what section of the country Tranter hailed from. The new deputy, in Dorne's not unconsidered judgment, had the look of a tough hombre. He looked to be the kind of man who lived by his wits, rather than the sweat of honest toil—to be exact, like a Rider of the Hungry Loop and Ready Cinch Ring. It was a fraternity which Dorne, when he took his oath of office, had sworn to rout. And he meant to do so with Tranter's aid.

Tranter might, of course, be just a drifting leather-slapper. He sure could slap it, Dorne reflected, like nobody's business. Yes, all things considered, he believed the new deputy was going to be a good man to have around. If he could only meet up with another drifting gunslammer open to the argument of good wages in exchange for a little sleight-of-hand, he opined he'd have this town plumb gentled inside a week.

It was with this thought in mind that Bill Dorne was suddenly brought up short in his stroll by the advent of a be-chapped and spurred buckaroo who had just bulged unexpectedly from the doorway of Manuel Venta's Broken Harp Saloon and gambling joint.

Dorne stared at the man, and the fellow stared back. There was an expectant look in this stranger's eyes that made Bill pause. The man had collided with him and, had Bill not been a cat on his feet, both of them would have gone down in a heap. Now the fellow seemed waiting and cocked for some sign of resentment from Bill.

Bill gave none. He just stood there hipshot, looking the other in the face. And the face was none too handsome, either. It was an ugly, jeering face, packing a knife-scar that ran from chin to ear along the left side. A face that held the pale, intense eyes of a killer. But a face, none the less, having a high, broad forehead denoting intelligence. The face of a man who had seen better days. That he was from the north—Colorado, Wyoming, Nebraska or the Dakotas—was evidenced by his goat-skin chaps; things much too hot and itchy for this part of the country.

"Wal, why don'tcha say it?" the fellow jeered.

"Say what?"

"Aw—hell! They sure raise 'em panty-waisted

round this here stretch of cact—" the fellow began. And ended. For just there, Bill's right fist—coming up from his bootstraps—took him under the chin and stretched him flat on his back, spreadeagled neatly across the plank walk.

Bill reached down with a long left hand, which he snagged in the fellow's shirt-front, and hoisted him to his feet as though he'd been a child. Bill let go and, before the fellow could fall, struck him a second pile-driver blow beneath the ear. The man in the hairy pants folded up without sound.

Bill heard the thud of booted feet and knew a crowd would be collecting fast. So, reaching down with both hands this time, he picked the fellow up, deposited him over one shoulder and started for the jail.

The place where Spavined Nag was wont to incarcerate its unruly citizens was a small adobe building to the rear of the Sheriff's Office. Towards this place Bill now packed the luckless buckaroo. A group of curious townsmen followed along at a discreet interval until Bill, with a fearful scowl, spun round on a heel and said: *"Git!"*

At which the curious *got,* and stood not upon the order of their getting, but got at once—complete and final. Bill grinned as he swung round and resumed his interrupted cruise toward jail.

Tranter saw him coming and met Bill before the Sheriff's Office.

"What'n seventeen purple prairie chickens you

got there? A hair mattress? Or is it a new kinda caterpillar?"

"Ain't right sure," Bill Dorne grunted. "But I aim to find out. Shall I take him into the office or dump him in the jail?"

"If yo're askin' me, I vote yuh bring 'im in the office," Tranter said. "Seems like I've met that coot before, someplace or other. I got a great mem'ry fer faces," he added solemnly. "I can even recollect the fella what baptized me when I was two weeks ol'. A big fella he was, with fiery red whiskers an' a black patch over one eye. He was a great fella fer swappin' jokes. I recall as how he tol' me one about the—"

"Save it for some other time," Bill cut him short. "Right now, we got to learn who this hellion is an' where he's drifted from. He's got a mean eye."

Tranter said, "What happened to him? Did 'e get shot? Or what? Where'd yuh find 'im, anyhow?"

"On the sidewalk front of the Broken Harp."

"Sleepin' off a drunk—"

"Sleepin' off a good sock on the jaw I gave him," Bill Dorne snapped. "By cripes, how long you think I'm gonna stand here holdin' him? Git out of the way so's I can take him inside."

Tranter moved, preceding Bill and his burden into the office, where Bill dumped the latter on the floor in front of his desk, thereby eliciting from the luckless northerner a doleful groan. Seconds later the fellow opened his eyes cautiously, blinked, winced and came to an elbow. "My Gawd!" he muttered. "You got a fist, Mister, that packs a slug like a shot of hundred proof! Don't hit me no more—I couldn't stand it. I ain't had a square meal in a week."

"What did you get thrown out of that saloon for? Tryin' to rob it?"

"Rob yore gran'mother! I was tryin' tuh bum me somethin' to eat!"

"Well, you'd ought to 'a' looked where you was lettin 'em pitch you. I've a good mind to throw you in jail for shootin' off your mouth the way you did. I'm waitin' for your apology."

"You sure got it," the Long-Faster said with alacrity. "I don't want no more argyments with *you!*" He stood rubbing his jaw tenderly with one hand, while cautiously caressing the bump behind his ear with the other. He eyed Bill Dorne reproachfully. "Whatja hit me with, anyhow—a hawsshoe?"

Bill Dorne grinned. "Them was just love pats I gave you," he chuckled. "Bear with me for a bit till I get warmed up an' I'll show you some hittin' as will make yore eyes bulge out!"

"No thanks. I know w'en tuh quit," the buckaroo protested vociferously. "This is the toughest burg I ever struck. What I'm needin', Mister, is a square meal. I ain't had nawthin' ter eat fer six days. Golly Moses but I'm hungry. Why—I'm so danged hungry I could eat a skunk an' like 'im!"

"Folks in this here town has tuh work fer their grub!" Tranter growled righteously. "We don't want no bums round here!"

Dorne grinned a little. Then he said to the stranger, "What handle do you pack?"

"I'm most generally known as Tumbleweed," said the man in the hairy chaps.

"Tumbleweed, eh?" Dorne considered. "Well, Tumble, can you manipulate that Peacemaker you got stashed in yore holster?"

"I sabe which end the smoke comes outa."

"Whereabouts do you hail from, Brother?" Tranter popped a question.

The drifting buckaroo slapped his pale-eyed glance on Tranter disapprovingly. "Where I come from folks don't ask strangers that kinda question—not onless they're lookin' for a fast grave. Further, Mister, they have learned in my part of the country that them that don't ast no questions, don't git told no blasted lies."

"Now listen, fella," Bill broke in earnestly. "Unless you're wantin' to spend time in my calaboose, then you better answer all questions we see fit to ask. I'm the Sheriff of this county, an' Tranter here is Chief Deputy. We—"

"Glad ter know yer, gents," Tumbleweed butted in. "Can either of yer spare a dime?"

Tranter snorted. "You got some nerve—"

"I got some speed, too!" Tumbleweed purred, and Tranter found himself staring down the muzzle of this stranger's short-barrelled .45. That this was an unprecedented situation for Tranter was evidenced by the way his eyes bulged out and the slackness manifested in the longitudinal position of his lower jaw. Dorne, too, stared at this drifting buckaroo in amaze. If Tranter was fast—and he most certainly was—then this belligerent Tumbleweed shamed lightning by comparison.

"Balance of the power is now vested in the minority," Tumbleweed drawled wickedly. "Empty out yore pockets, gents, an' empty 'em pronto onless yer wants ter view the daisies from a worm's altytood!"

Dorne and Tranter exchanged chagrined glances. This was pretty bad. Stuck up by a hairy-pantsed stranger right in the Sheriff's own office! If the town ever got wind of this they'd be the laughing stocks of the whole county. Unless they could swiftly get the upper hand.

"Shell out, gents! Shell out an' make it snappy! Why, yer pore deluded gophers! There ain't no man alive can sock Tumbleweed Shane under the button an' behind the ear, an' git away with it. Nor there ain't no ragbag on Gawd's green footstool what kin sneer down his nose at me!" His pale, killer eyes glared fiercely. "Shell out, yer dang tin-belly star-packers!"

Bill and Tranter turned their pockets inside out; Bill philosophically, Tranter with unconcealed malignance. "He what laffs last—" Tranter began.

But Tumbleweed's hoarse chuckle cut him off. "Wall, I'm doin' the laffin', sonny, an'—"

But Tumbleweed's words and Tumbleweed's laughter both abruptly ceased together as Bill Dorne's booted foot came up like the sun out of China, batted the pistol out of his hand and sent it spinning across the room. Before it landed, Tumbleweed was gazing viciously into the gaping bore of Tranter's hog-leg.

"The worm has turned," Tranter sneered, and spat at a knothole a scant half inch from Tumbleweed's left boot. "What'll we do with this ingrate, Bill?"

"What we'd ought to do by rights," Bill said, "is shove him in the jail an' forget about 'im." He stared resentfully at the glaring Tumbleweed. "What was the big idea?"

Tumbleweed's scowl vanished in a sudden grin. "Jest havin' a little fun with you boys, that's all. Wanted ter see if I could beat yer to the draw." He chuckled. "It was like takin' candy from a kid."

"Yeah?" said Tranter, advancing with an oath. "Well, if I swipe this gun's muzzle acrost yore homely mug yuh won't be thinkin' it's so dang funny, I'm bettin'!"

"Hold on, Buck," Dorne interposed, picking up his belongings and stuffing them back in his pockets. "Do you want a job, Tumble—a good job that packs excitement an' forty bucks a month?"

"Where is it?" Tumbleweed looked sceptical.

"Right here," Bill explained. "I need another deputy an' you sure got all the signs of makin' just the kind I'm lookin' for. What do you say?"

Tumbleweed appeared to consider, rasping a none-too-clean hand across his stubbly jaw. At last he admitted, "Wal, I might sort of give it a whirl."

"Good," said Bill, and swore him in, Tranter looking on disgustedly. Bill then gave his new deputy some money and told him to go out and fill his aching cavity. When he had gone, Tranter growled lugubriously:

"Jest pilin' up trouble for us, that's what you're doin'. That li'l scorpion's plumb cultus, if I know the breed! Yuh should've put yore heel on 'im, Bill. He'll live tuh sting us yet."

V / JOB FOR A BUCKAROO

An hour or so later when Tumbleweed returned, it was to find Bill Dorne comfortably tilted back in a chair behind the Sheriff's desk, with his spurred boots reclining inelegantly upon its much-pitted surface. Tranter had left the office, having been sent by Dorne to keep an eye on the resorts which already were dusting off their tables and polishing up their glasses for the evening trade.

Dorne said, "Take a chair, Tumble. We're gonna *habla* a spell."

Tumbleweed pulled up a chair and perched himself gingerly upon the extreme edge. He looked enquiringly at the sheriff.

"What kind of work do you do? I mean," Dorne elucidated, "what's yore profession—cowpuncher, buckaroo—"

"That's it."

"What?"

"Buckaroo," said Tumbleweed succinctly.

Bill Dorne let his blue-eyed glance play over his newest deputy in a manner that was closely speculative. "Work on the theory that a man who wastes no words wastes no breath, and that silence is worth its weight in gold, I reckon," he commented. "Now s'pose you loosen up a mite an' get confidential. Where'd you work last as a rider?"

"Box O B, Salty Crick, Nevada."

"Never heard of it."

"Wal," grunted Tumbleweed with a sly smile, "I reckon even the Sheriff of Spavined Nag ain't heard of ever'thin'."

Bill snorted, and eyed the hairy-chapped man more closely. "There's more to you than meets the eye," he opined drily. "So you worked for the Box O B. What kind of monicker did you give the ramrod for a last name to stick on his payroll?"

"Tumbleweed—just plain Tumbleweed. I ain't one of them high-minded aristocrats what has to have two handles to git called to grub with. Plain Tumbleweed's good enough for me."

"Yeah. Tumbleweed, eh? Ever been a bronc peeler, Tumble?"

"Oh, I've gentled two-three rough 'uns in my time," the new deputy admitted modestly. "How come all this curiosity? If I might ast?"

"Vital statistics for the Sheriff's Office," Dorne answered. "We have to know who we got workin' for us, an' why." The blue of Dorne's eyes grew thoughtful as he sat regarding his newest deputy, who was softly whistling a tune the while his pale eyes roved the raftered ceiling. "You're pretty fast at gettin' out that hog-leg you're totin'. Ever hire it out?"

"Yer mean am I a perfeshional gun slinger?" Tumbleweed queried innocently. And at Dorne's nod, "Hell, no—I'm a buckaroo, like I told yer."

"Let it go," Dorne said. "Where'd you work before you got that job at the Box O B?"

"Deer Lodge—I was workin' fer the government."

"I see," Bill said, though he didn't. But he decided not to push his questions any further in that direction before this man who had worked for the government, for fear of making himself appear ignorant of Sheriff procedure. Instead he said, "Can you read sign?"

"Shucks, that ain't my long suit," Tumbleweed admitted with a wry grin. "To tell yer the truth, I couldn't find a baseball in a termato can."

Bill thought awhile in silence. When he spoke, finally, it was in a greatly lowered voice. He was a great believer in the saw that even walls have ears. "I'm going," he said, "to give you a risky job. But it's an important one an' I hope you won't turn it down."

"What kinda job?" Tumbleweed asked suspiciously. "I hear that yer done ordered Borst ter get shut of this town. Don't give me no job seein' that he gets shut of it, because I wouldn't be able ter git very enthusiastic about a chore o' that kind."

"Listen," Bill said earnestly. "What I want you to do is go over to Borst an' hit him for a job," and he looked at Tumbleweed intently.

Tumbleweed looked back, and just as intently, between his suddenly narrowed lids.

Bill said softly, "Do you get it?"

"'Fraid I don't. Better chew it finer."

"What I want you to do," said Bill briefly, "is to get on Borst's payroll where you'll have a chance to work yoreself into his good graces an' be in a position to act as undercover man for this office."

"Thought yer was orderin' Borst outa town?"

"I am. But I got a notion he ain't figgerin' to go very far."

"Wal, I don't wanta be no sneakin' spy!"

"Don't be a fool. What I'm offerin' you is a damned important job; it's a compliment to yore ability that I'm even askin' you to take it. An' the pay'll be sixty bucks a month. If you keep yore head the chances of you bein' caught will be pretty slim."

"Yeah—an' so'll my chances of gettin' out with a whole skin if I *do* git caught!" Tumbleweed snorted. "What do yer think I am? You got me mixed up with some other gent, Mister. Me, I ain't cut out ter be no martyr. I got a few things I want ter do yet afore I pass in my checks."

"Eighty," said Bill softly.

"Not on yer tinpipe!"

"A hundred."

"Huh? What's that?" Tumbleweed whispered. "Say that ag'in."

"A hundred bucks per month if you can cut it."

"Cripes!" Tumbleweed muttered, and: "I reckon I'm the world's champeen nit-wit ter even think about it. But . . . a hundred bucks per month—Hell, I'll take yer up on that." Tumbleweed's leathery face was very solemn.

Bill shook his hand and got to his feet. "Fine," he said, simply. "Keep me posted."

Tumbleweed paused at the door and turned. "How would yer suggest that I go about gettin' this job with Borst? Is he lookin' fer some help?"

"Couldn't say. But he owns a ranch—cattle ranch—besides this dive in town. He oughta be able to use a good tough hand."

"Thanks," Tumbleweed said, and grinned. "Leave it ter me; I'll git on."

As he went out the door Tranter came in. There was a disapproving scowl on the ragged deputy's face. He put a hand to his nose and walked around in a circle. Then, stopping before Dorne, he shook his head. "Them as sups with the devil sure needs a long spoon."

"What you talkin' about?"

"You an' that two-legged polecat what jest went out. Don't never let it be said I didn't warn yuh! You'll get yore tail in a sling yet, foolin' with that hombre."

Dorne got out his pipe and filled its bowl. He lit it and inhaled gratefully. Then, expelling the smoke from his nostrils, he looked at Tranter closely. "What you so down on that fella for?"

"Don't like 'im," Tranter grunted shortly. "He's plumb cultus. You take it from a man what knows.

I wish to hell I could recollect where I seen him before. It wa'n't no place good, I'll swear."

"What's wrong with him?"

"How in seven devils do I know?" Tranter demanded testily. "But he's a bad 'un. Didja git a look at his eyes?"

Bill grunted. "Trouble is with you, you're jealous. I told Tumble to get himself a job with Borst. He's goin' to be our undercover man."

"Yeah? Wal," Tranter scowled, "there's no fool like a young 'un. Speakin' of Borst, he's done moved. Pulled out bag an' baggage not ten minutes ago. I'm s'prised he fell for yore bluff."

"That wasn't no bluff," Bill said. "If he hadn't gone I'd have seen that he was carried out on a shutter. When I say somethin' I mean business. Borst knows it an' acted accordin'."

"Oh, yeah? Wal, that's one way of lookin' at it. I met yore preacher while I was at supper. Seems right discouraged. Called this place a sink of iniquity an'—"

"That sky-pilot's a pretty good egg. Only he's kinda impatient. Rome wasn't built in a day."

"That's what I told him," Tranter said. "He says as how he's been a-labourin' in this Lord's vineyard for goin' on six months an' ain't gathered one grape yet. He's pretty down in the mouth."

Leaving the Sheriff's office, Tumbleweed crossed the street and went into the place recently occupied by the Golden Stack. Finding the place empty, he came out again and asked a passing puncher, "What happened ter Borst?"

"Sheriff bluffed him outa town," said the puncher. "Claims he's goin' to open up in the old Seldies place. Reckon you'll find him out there if yore business is urgent."

Tumbleweed wheeled and headed for the stable where he got his horse, and swinging into the worn saddle he had not bothered to take off, forked him out of town at a quick jog.

It was almost dark when he reached the Seldies place. He could see it as soon as he had topped the first rise after leaving town, for the place was a blaze of light as Borst's men rushed to get it into order for the night's business, which he plainly expected to follow him to his new location. Guided by its beckoning windows, Tumbleweed located it without difficulty or further directions. Dismounting before the old place, he tied his horse—a hammer-headed roan—to the newly and hastily erected hitching rail, and clumped his spurs inside.

Borst's men had been working fast. The bar was in and the mirror set along the wall behind it. Three sweating bartenders were unpacking the bottled goods. The tinhorns were getting their games in readiness and a couple of swampers were sweeping the bar-room out, while six carpenters were swiftly putting down a dance floor in the room behind it. Two more carpenters were busily engaged, amid much cussing, in enlarging the connecting doorway.

Pausing a few moments, Tumbleweed surveyed these activities with a keen interest. Then he tightened the slack in his belt, spat on his hands and, rubbing them across his hairy chaps, went swaggering over to one of the gamblers.

"Borst around?" he asked.

The gambler nodded his sleek black head without bothering to look up. "Yeah—back room. The door on the right. An' you better knock."

But evidently Tumbleweed was not accustomed to knocking upon doors, for he entered the room indicated without troubling with such formality. There was a girl with Borst. A girl with vivid green eyes in a pale face framed by golden hair. Lola.

Borst looked up with a scowl. "What do you want?"

"A talk with yer."

Borst looked him over carefully. Then he said to the girl "Git," and she went out. Borst's smoke-grey eyes swung back to Tumbleweed. "Spill it."

"I been wonderin' could yer use another hand."

"What's yore line?"

"Anythin' the other gents won't tackle."

"Hard guy, eh?" said Borst, with a glint of amusement in his look.

"I ain't makin' no brags," said Tumbleweed

easily, "but I'm allus willin' ter demonstrate—allus hev been an' I allus will."

The boss of Spavined Nag permitted a grin to reach his thick-lipped mouth. "Sort of handy man, eh?"

"Allus hev been, an' there's a pretty good chanct I allus will. Don't you reckon?"

Borst's sleepy lids shut down a bit. "Couldn't say. What kinda job d'you want?"

Tumbleweed rasped his chin. "I ain't speshully partic'lar—jest so's there's plenty of dinero in it."

"Have you met our new sheriff? His name's Bill Dorne."

"I've seen him," a grimace crossed Tumbleweed's ugly face. "He's knowed as *Wild* Bill Dorne."

"Well, I might be able to use you," Borst said, looking him over. "I could use you all right if you could get yoreself a job in the Sheriff's Office. There would be good money in it, too. Money from here an' money from there. Do you think you could cut it?" Borst's eyes were on Tumbleweed's sharply as he asked the question.

Tumbleweed grinned and, taking his left hand from his pocket, laid a bit of metal carefully on the desk in front of the big resort keeper. A touch of deeper colour came into Borst's beefy face. He straightened, still looking at that object Tumbleweed had set before him. Then his glinting glance flashed to Tumbleweed's face.

"You're hired," he said, and chuckled.

Tumbleweed chuckled, too.

When Tumbleweed had taken his departure, Borst called Gleed, the bouncer, into the back room. Gleed looked hot and sweaty. He had been working with the others, hurrying to get this new location of the Golden Stack ready for a celebration Borst had ordered in honour of the change.

Borst said, "If Bill Dorne comes out here tonight, let him be. My orders, for the present, are hands off. Sabe? Right now Bill Dorne is goin' to be a durned sight more use to me alive than dead."

Gleed looked back at him curiously. Then he shrugged his gorilla shoulders and a sneer slid across the lips beneath his broken nose. "Yer gettin' soft," he jeered. "Y'oughta join the Panty-waist Club. Cripes, it fair makes my liver crawl ter see yer knuckle under to thet blasted Billy-be-Damned Dorne. What's—"

"That's enough outa you," Borst purred. "I'm runnin' this, savvy? An' what I say goes. An' I don't want no lip from you! Get me?"

Gleed nodded with a surly grimace. "It's yer funeral."

"Funeral—hell! If there's any plantin' goin' to be done, I'll be the guy to do it. Bill Dorne has seen his best days, an' you can stick a pin in that. I'm takin' care of him when the sign's right. You do what I tell you an' you an' me will get along fine. When you go back outside you can pass the word around. All hands are to lay off Dorne until I give the word."

Gleed left the room and Lola returned. Borst looked up from some papers he was sorting. "Listen," he said heavily, "you get hold of Bill Dorne an' keep him busy to-night—"

"What about my game?" cut in Lola.

"To hell with yore game! Someone else can tend to it. Yore job's to find Bill Dorne pronto, an' to keep him in tow for the rest of the night."

VI / *SCORE ONE FOR THE SPORTING ELEMENT*

It was some time after old mother night had draped her sable folds across the town of Spavined Nag that Bill Dorne put on his hat and left the Sheriff's Office with Buck Tranter for a tour around the various resorts fronting the main street. Business was good and all hands seemed busy whooping it up. This was a payday night, and plenty of punchers were in from the outlying ranches, boisterous, exuberant, and as willing to fight as to drink.

"Goin' to be a kind of tough night," Dorne remarked to Tranter, and did not dream that his words were to come so true as the morrow was to prove them.

Tranter nodded sagely. "Yuh shore said somethin' that time. It's goin' tuh be a thirsty night, too. An' all these punchers bulgin' intuh town ain't goin' tuh be satisfied till they've raised hell an' shoved a chunk under it. My advice, young fella, is tuh let 'em do it. An' keep plumb outen the way, so's it won't git dropped on yore pet corn."

"These joints are gonna have to close up by two o'clock," Bill growled. "That's long enough for any gent to work the Old Adam out of his system."

Tranter got out his plug of tobacco and bit off a

generous chew. "Well," he opined drily, "you're the doctor, I reckon. She's yore game an' I guess yuh kin play 'er as yuh please. But if I was you, I'd let these joints plumb alone to-night. Depend upon it; that's comin' from a man what knows! This is yore cue tuh step soft an' easy fer a spell. Yuh've run Borst out of town—don't try crowdin' yore luck too far."

Bill reached out abruptly and put a hand on Tranter's arm. "Wait a minute," he muttered. And Tranter, following the direction of his glance, saw a woman coming toward them through the jostling crowd. A girl, in fact. Lola. Men were backing aside right and left to let her pass, and looking after her with admiring glances.

Tranter snorted. "I thought I heard yuh was engaged tuh be married!"

Bill made no answer, but his cheeks got red. He kept his eyes on Lola, and there was a keen interest in them.

But not in Tranter's. "I'll be amblin' along," he grunted.

"All right," Bill said. "I'll see you later. Better make the rounds of these places an' see that there ain't no rough stuff." He did not look at Tranter; he was too busy admiring Lola's lithe swinging form. He was still admiring it when she came up with that grave smile she seemed to reserve for him alone. "Hello, Bill Dorne," she said.

"Howdy, Lola. Doin' the town?"

"Not really. Just out for a breath of air. One of the boys is taking my game for awhile. How's the sheriffing business? Who was that range tramp you were talking with?"

"That's my new deputy," Bill said, gazing after the departing Tranter with a grin. "I reckon he's kinda woman-shy. He cut his stick soon's he seen you comin'. If you ain't busy, what say we take in the sights?"

"We-ll," she appeared reluctant, but let Bill hold her hand. "Perhaps we'd better not. After all," she smiled, "you're engaged to be married now."

"I ain't married yet," Bill said. "Come on," and linked his arm in hers. "How'd you get to town?" he asked after a few silent moments of battling their way through the crowded streets. "Didn't you move out with the rest of yore crowd to Borst's new stand?"

"Yes. One of the cowboys lent me his horse for the evening. I've left it at the livery."

They walked along in silence for a spell—silence on their part, that is. For the night itself was anything but quiet. Raucous voices called the figures of reels and jigs to the scrape of fiddles, the twanging of guitars, and the reedy notes of a windy mouth organ. Feet stamped in time. These sounds were only a background for other, nearer, sounds. Oaths, snatches of ribald tales, occasional guffaws and once a woman's high-pitched laughter.

Bill did not seem to be heading toward any of the resorts. Neither did he appear to be strolling aimlessly. Lola must have observed that they were walking toward the edge of town. But it wasn't the edge where the Globe house was situated. So she offered no protest. Content, apparently, just being in Bill's company. Her fingers made soft pressure as they lay inside Bill's bigger ones. The night was hot, but there was a cool wind springing up off the desert, and as their sauntering took them further from the noise of those boisterous pleasure-seekers, they could hear the steady chirping of the crickets.

They had reached a spot by now some hundreds of yards from the edge of town. Spavined Nag's garish lights did not spoil the night's beauty out here. Not if one faced the other way.

The dark eerie forms of tall sajuarro made darker patterns against the desert's thinning black. Patterns appearing to fill this girl beside him with some vague dread or sense of disquietude. For she pressed closer to him and, before Bill knew it—or realized what the night and this girl's proximity were doing to him—he found his arms around her. Tight. And his lips on hers, and hers returning their pressure vividly.

Buck Tranter, with his Chief Deputy's star glinting proudly from its perch on the left breast of his patched orange flannel shirt, making his rounds of Spavined Nag's resorts, was being received with an apparent respect and cordiality that was surely royal. Never in all his long and checkered career had he been so wined and fêted as he was this night.

Seemed like every dive he visited he was made to feel more welcome. At first he could not understand all this friendly interest, but after the twentieth glass had dropped its fiery contents down his throat, he made up his mind that he was quite a mixer and let it go at that.

At Ortega's Black Bottle Bar he was served the best on the shelf, and later invited to take a hand in a stud game that was in progress. The stakes were pretty steep and he sort of shook his head and opined that it was a wise man who knew when to let well enough alone. But after a bit of coaxing, he was wheedled into playing for about a long half hour. At the end of which time he got up from the table wealthier by three hundred dollars. And felt pretty slick.

At Venta's Broken Harp he was asked to swig from Venta's private bottle. Which he did with pleasure and much smacking of the lips. It was prime stuff, he allowed. And was given a bottle to carry with him—in case he got to feeling dry between stops.

At Venta's, too, he took a whirl at the wheel. Elated at a hundred dollar win, he let his money ride and doubled it. Again he left it on the board, and once again he doubled it. Other players were beginning to follow his leads and there was a ring three deep sweating the game when he finally raked in his profits, and with bulging, clinking pockets left the place.

He stopped for a spell in two-three smaller joints and emerged amply repaid for the pause. Standing outside the swinging doors of the last place, he scratched his shaggy head and stood groggily watching the noisy punchers trooping by. How long he stood there would be hard to tell, but finally, biting off a huge chew from his plug of Brown's Mule, he went masticating toward the livery stable at a more or less rolling gait.

The stable's proprietor was a handsome gent. And very obliging. He got out Tranter's flea-bitten crow-bait, gave it a rub and saddled it for him. And wouldn't take a tip. Moreover, had Tranter been strictly sober instead of slightly pie-eyed, he would have found some cause to wonder at the ridiculously low fee he was charged for the two-day care of his horse.

But he wasn't strictly sober after all the libations that had burned their way downward past his gullet. He slapped the stable-keeper on the back in jovial gusto, called him a good sport and handed him one of the cigars that had been pressed upon him as he made his rounds. Then, right pleased with himself and the rest of the world, he kicked his decrepit-looking nag in the ribs and pointed its head toward the Seldies place, three miles out on the desert.

Tranter crawled off his bonerack nag in front of the new Golden Stack and, not bothering to trail his reins or tie them, dragged his spurs inside. Things were pretty lively. Booted and belted buckaroos were whirling thinly-draped females round the dance floor at a most reckless pace, stamping on one another's toes to the fiddles' wail of Turkey in the Straw. The games, he could see, were well patronized and the long bar was lined with men four deep. As usual, it appeared, the Golden Stack—even though removed three miles from town—was getting the lion's share of business.

Tranter had hardly weaved his way inside the swinging doors when the bullet-headed, broken-nosed Gleed came striding forward, a grin stretching across his ugly map from ear to cauliflowered ear, and grasped Buck joyously by the hand. With his free paw he slapped Buck's shoulder.

Tranter gasped: "Hey! Dammit! Don't shake m' teeth plumb out. Ack civilized, can't yuh? Whatcha think this is? An' m' hand ain't no dang pump handle. So lay off'n it, fella. Lemme get m' breath!"

"Ain't you ol' Slip-Shot Tranter?" asked Gleed, as though surprised.

"Hell, yes! An' what ef I am?" demanded

Tranter belligerently. "I kin lick m' weight in wildcats, an'll sieve the guy what says I can't!"

"Wal, they ain't no gent here what'll say so," Gleed assured him, grinning. "It sure warms the cockles of my heart to see you here in Spavined Nag, Slip-Shot. Gonna drop yore picket pin a spell?" And at Tranter's nod, Gleed's jaw abruptly dropped in simulated amazement. "Gosh! Fer the love o' Lizzie! Have you done reformed?"

Tranter's bleary eyes followed Gleed's hard gaze to the star pinned on the front of his shirt. "What'cha mean, reformed?"

"You shore didn't pack no star in the old days—"

"Naw. I'm jest wearin' this tin badge tuh show a coupla incredulous gents that ol' Buck Tranter can be any damn thing he wants."

Gleed chuckled. "Like any old fool could doubt it! C'mon, have a drink, Buck, fer ol' time's sake."

"Wal, I don't care ef I do," grunted Buck, and permitted the grinning Gleed to pilot him up to the bar. When they had downed three-four drinks— "to get the alkali out of their systems" as Gleed put it—Gleed led Tranter over to a poker game. And with a flick of his off eye, got a chair vacated for Buck so quick he never noticed that a man had been sitting there as they came up.

When Tranter finally quit the Golden Stack some three hours later he didn't have two coins left to clink together.

• • •

And, during this same evening, out on the range where the Wineglass cattle ran, a group of shadowy, swift-working, horsebacked figures cautiously hazed all of Mayor Globe's two-year-olds that could be found without much dalliance, off along a trail that ran south toward the Mexican Border—the trail of no return. And these cattle were not what might be described by a Westerner as a little jag of beef; this was a wholesale manoeuvre, designed to break Globe quick.

And in town things were going on, too—things seen by neither Dorne nor Tranter. Things which Borst had no intention of allowing to reach their ears. Till the harvest was gathered, and his share salted away.

It was after two when Bill Dorne rolled into his bunk in the room behind the Sheriff's Office. The two saloons, he knew, had not closed at two. But right then he had too much else on his mind to care. And was to have a good deal more.

VII / "EEF YOU ARE LOOK FOR TROUBLE—"

When Bill Dorne returned from an early breakfast the next morning, he found Buck Tranter seated in his chair and with his spurred heels hooked atop the desk.

"Hey," Bill growled. "Get yore dang feet down off'n there! What do you think this is?"

Tranter chewed in a morose silence for a while, then observed, "I've seen you sittin' this here way."

"What of it? *I'm* the sheriff!"

"Wal," said Tranter, and spat at a knothole across the room, "I'm the sheriff's helper."

Bill Dorne's face made a grimace. "A hell of a helper *you* are! Why didn't you close up them saloons an' gamblin' dives last night at two o'clock, like I told you to?"

"Yuh didn't tell me to. Yuh say as how yuh aimed for them tuh be closed by that time; but yuh never said I was tuh do the closin'. An' if yuh had," Tranter added flatly, "I'd 'a' tole yuh to yore face that yuh couldn't hire me tuh try pullin' no dumb stunt like that. Besides, these here fellas what runs them joints is plumb friendly towards me. The—"

"Friendly as a Gila Monster," Dorne said sarcastically. "Don't never trust the sportin' element in this man's town, 'cause they'll knife you every time. I ought to know. I've spent quite some time hangin' round them joints—before I got to be sheriff, that is. That fella Borst would just as leave order yore throat cut as order you a drink."

"Yeah—an' a whole lot liefer!" Tranter growled. "I went intuh his place about two-thirty with my pockets stuffed with money. Musta had three-four thousand dollars on me—"

"Three-four *what!*"

"Thousand dollars," snapped Tranter emphatically. "I'd been takin' them other dives down the road. But them fellas up at Borst's musta seen me comin', 'cause they shore had their axe out. An' brother, was it sharp! In three hours they cleaned me down to a dime! An' I thought I knew a thing or two about poker!"

"You dang fool," Bill said. "You'd oughta known better'n that."

"Yeah—that's what the alligator said when he took the swimmer's laig off!" Tranter regarded him slantways. "Speakin' of fools; I ain't the on'y one in these parts."

Bill, on his way to the water-cooler for a drink, swung suddenly round. "What exactly was the meanin' of that?"

"Wal, I guess yuh know. An' if yuh don't well then jest ferget it," Tranter said, and turned to look out the window. "There's some fella hot-footin' it this way like he was in a big hurry. Know 'im?"

Bill came over to take a look, and swore. "Hell, yes! That's Fisk—president of the Stockman's Bank."

Fisk came in panting.

"What's up?"

Fisk said, "Plenty!" and looked as though he meant it. "Somebody robbed the bank last night. I went in to open up, an' there was the vault door standin' open an' papers strewn all over the floor. They got every bit of currency. An' most of the silver. The gold, thank God, they didn't find."

Bill looked at Tranter and Tranter looked at Bill. Then Bill pursed his lips in a soundless whistle. And began to look proddy.

"Ain't that somethin'!" Tranter said.

Bill growled, "When'd it happen? How'd they get in? How come they didn't get the gold?"

Fisk grunted, "Last night some time, I suppose. Sawed the bars off one of the back windows an' busted in the glass. I had the gold cached in another place. And damn lucky. This robbery's goin' to put an awful dent in us, Sheriff. I think we can weather it. But it'll be a mighty close shave."

"Got any idea who done it?" Tranter asked.

Fisk glared at him. "What d'you suppose I came over here for? You gents have been put in office to apprehend criminals. Not to ask a passle of fool questions. What are you waitin' around for?"

"C'mon," Bill growled to Tranter, and led the way toward the bank, which was down the street five or six doors. Fisk strode angrily after them, muttering to himself.

They entered the bank, Bill's rolling shoulders shoving a way through the crowd collected about the open doorway.

Tranter glared at the crowd. "What in seven blue devils you guys standin' round here for? Close yore mouths an' take 'em with yuh ter some other climate. *Git!*" he said, and reached for his gun.

With resentful growls the crowd broke up.

As Fisk had said, the interior was strewn with papers, ledgers, day books, securities, and here and there the contents of envelopes had been scattered as though the looters had pawed through them hurriedly.

"I'd say," Tranter remarked, looking round, "that a Kansas twister'd been in here."

Fisk scowled. "This is no time for pleasantries," he declared icily. "What I want to know is what you fellows are goin' to do about it?"

"Keep yore shirt on," Dorne said. "We'll get to the bottom of this business. May take a little time. But we'll get there. You can stick a pin in that!"

He looked into the littered vault whose door had been opened with nitro-glycerine. "How much exactly has been taken?"

Fisk ran worried hands through his thatch of

silver grey hair. "My God!" he groaned. "I can't tell offhand. Round forty thousand, I'd say roughly."

Tranter whistled.

"Pretty much dinero for a bank of this size to be carryin', ain't it?"

"This was payday night. Two or three ranchers just sold herds. Had a small shipment of dust from the Topekas Mine. We were aiming to send it to the capital this morning."

Dorne nodded. "Well, we'll do what we can. I'd like to look around now for clues."

For a solid hour Dorne and Tranter probed about, but their search availed them nothing. Then Tranter asked, "Whyn't yuh look fer fingerprints? I hear they're ketchin' plenty of hard cases that way now."

But Dorne shook his head. "This office ain't equipped for that. Besides, what I don't know about fingerprintin' would fill a volume. C'mon. We'll make a round of the saloons. Mebbe someone heard the blast. They used nitroglycerine to get that vault door off. Somebody oughta heard that explosion."

But though they canvassed the town systematically, questioned people adroitly, all they found was one man who "thought" he'd heard an explosion of some sort about three o'clock. He'd been sleeping off a jag in the alley back of the bank.

"This is a hell of a sitcheation," Tranter growled. "How'n heck we gonna ketch this bank-robbin' party when we ain't even got a reliable witness to the time, an' there ain't no clues?"

Dorne nodded. "The sum total of our knowledge is absolutely nothin'," he agreed morosely. "But we'll get that robber—we got to! You keep yore ears peeled, Buck. Sooner or later we'll find out somethin'. Bound to. The law of averages."

"Must be a new law," Tranter opined. "I hadn't heard of it before."

Dorne flashed him a disgusted look. "C'mon, I'm servin' notice on these joints. Hereafter they're gonna close by two o'clock or I'll know the reason why."

Tranter picked up his hat. "You'll know, I reckon," he muttered drily.

They returned to the Sheriff's Office after making their announcement. It had not been kindly received, as Tranter had predicted. Scowls and smothered oaths had followed them from each successive resort they visited. "It's a ordinance of this town," Bill said, "an' by Jupiter, it's gonna be obeyed."

Tranter sat down on the edge of his desk and mopped his forehead with the back of a sleeve. "It sure is thirsty weather! Never see such a place fer onregenerated heat—it's enough tuh cook yore gizzard!"

Dorne frowned gloomily at the floor. "I'd give

somethin' to know who robbed that bank," he growled.

"So'd Fisk," Tranter chuckled. "It was a damn neat piece of work."

"I'm bettin' Borst had his hand in it," Dorne said grimly.

"You got Borst on the brain," Tranter said, and snorted.

"I—" Bill Dorne abruptly stopped and stared narrowly toward the door.

Tranter heard the clump and clink of spurred boots on the walk outside and followed Dorne's glance, just as one of Globe's cowboys stepped inside. His face was red and covered with powdered alkali and sweat, and there was a wild look in his eye.

"Listen, Dorne—listen!" he panted; "We lost a hundred an' fifty head of prime two-year-old Wineglass critters las' night!"

"Huh!" Dorne came out of his chair with a surge.

"So help me Hannah!" the puncher growled. "Rustlers worked our range an' ran off every two-year-old we got!"

"Didja see 'em?" Tranter asked. "Anybody hurt?"

"By cripes no, we didn't see 'em! They'd 'a' been somebody hurt all right if we had! One hundred an' fifty prime steers! By cripes, it's a outrage!"

"It sure is," Bill said, soothingly. "When'd you discover they was gone?"

"First thin' this mawnin' when we hit for the gatherin' ground. We been roundin' 'em up for a week. Globe's fit tuh be tied!"

"Let's get this straight," Bill said. "You been roundin' up two-year-olds for a shipment?" And, at the puncher's nod, "Then why wasn't a coupla nightherds ridin' circle?"

"They was!" the puncher said, and swore. "They was part of the gang, I reckon. They've hauled their freight—plumb vanished like our steers!"

"Names!" Bill snapped, reaching for a pad of paper. "An' description. We may be able to pull them jaspers in."

"Ed Krayston, tall, lanky, with a knife scar over his left blinker. An' Dode Harniss, a sawed-off gnat what needs a ladder tuh reach the chow table."

"Say," said Tranter, scratching his shaggy head. "I've met up with that Harniss gent before. He's a mean actor—plumb cultus, in fact."

"Good," said Bill. "You keep yore eye out for him. We'll run him in, first thing. Mebbe we can make him squeal on the rest of 'em."

"No chance," Tranter replied. "He's saltier'n Lot's wife."

"You ketch him," the puncher said, "an' I'll give him a workin' over that'll be right revealin'. I know a Injun trick or two what'll make that pelican holler calf-rope right sudden!"

"Did the rustlers leave any sign?"

"Hell, yes. The prairie's cut up plenty. Boys are trailin' 'em now. But they won't have no luck. You wait an' see. These fellers is slick. They been messin' round with us fer quite a spell, nibblin' off a few head here an' there. This is the first time they ever run off so big a jag, though. Must be gettin' ambition."

"Or mebbe," said Bill, "yore two missin' circle riders are the ones that were doin' the nibblin'. My guess is they've joined up with big-time company."

"Might be somethin' in that," Tranter agreed. "This Harniss hairpin, though, is a old hand. He sabes plenty, believe me. An' he can use a gun."

"So can my ol' man," the puncher grunted. "If Globe ever gets his hands on them gents, mince meat's gonna be coarse beside 'em!"

"If—" Tranter began, and stopped with his mouth still open as from across the street some place came the sudden crash of gunfire. The puncher stared at Tranter, and the ragged deputy stared back. Dorne swung round with an oath and, snatching up his hat, made for the door with catlike strides. Tranter and the Wineglass puncher whirled and followed.

The trio reached the street in time to see a man lurch staggering from the swinging doors of

Ortega's Black Bottle Bar. A whiskered desert rat. And there was a smoking pistol in one downswung hand as he backed stumblingly down the steps and into the dusty street. A stain was rapidly spreading on his shirt.

Dorne, running toward him, scrutinized him well. But did not recognize him as anyone he had seen before. Some stranger, evidently. He lengthened his stride.

Yet before he had covered more than half the distance across the street the doors of the Black Bottle bulged outward again. A man came crouching through them. A man with dark swarthy face wrinkled now in a malevolent grin. A face that held eyes that were tiny and alive with flashing sparkles—a Mexican's face, and one that Dorne knew well. The face of Pedro Mendota, one of Pecos Borst's ace gunslammers.

The white teeth of him showed now against his coppery skin in a tigerish smirk as he fired three times into the falling sage-brusher. And one more shot he threw in as the old fellow swayed, coughing blood, on hands and knees.

Dorne had an instant of tautness, and his face went pale as desert sand. Then he said, all at once laughing and reckless, "The brave Don Pedro has shot hisself a man!" And the scorn dripped from his words like a visible thing.

The Mexican faced him alertly, his swarthy face handsome despite the snarling curl of his tight-lipped mouth. The gun was still in his hand, but with a sudden show of bravado he thrust it in the flapless brass-studded holster that sagged the front of his belt.

Dorne's narrowed eyes held a steely glint. "Bold as Billy-be-damned, ain't you, Mendota? Specially when it's a broken-down ol' man you're pickin' on."

Fighting words. But Mendota laughed smooth and easy. "Thees fella, he draw first, *si*. You can ask the patrons in thees Black Bottle, if you no believe. But I am not making for back down, señor." The white teeth flashed in a sneer beneath his tiny black mustache. "Eef you are look for trouble, *por Dios*, I give you belly full!"

VIII / *THE ARKANSAS TOOTHPICK*

Dorne checked the rush of his lifting temper with difficulty. This Mendota always rubbed him the wrong way. Dorne hated his sneers and swaggering bravado. They had never cottoned to each other since that day, two months ago when—in defence of a drunken puncher—Bill Dorne had all but wiped up Borst's Golden Stack with the Mex gunman. Mendota, he had realized even then, was not the man to forgive such a public beating as Dorne had administered. Mendota had neither forgiven it nor forgotten it. And right now he seemed in a mood to even up the score. In his own way—with a pistol.

But though these things flashed through Bill Dorne's mind, no slightest indication of his feelings was permitted to show upon his lean bronzed cheeks. Bill's temper was a fearful thing, unleashed. But now he held it under firm control and, striding past the sneering gun fighter, he strode determinedly inside Ortega's Black Bottle Bar, the customers giving back before him, frightened perhaps by what they read in his narrowed eyes.

"That dawg out there says the old desert rat drew first. Can any gent corroborate that statement?" His voice was clipped and cold.

The even clump of boots and the jingle of

dragging spur chains told him that others had followed him inside. But Dorne flashed no look at the men who had crowded in behind him. All his attention was on this glowering crowd before him. Particularly on Jose Ortega, a crook-nosed fellow with a short, piratical spade beard.

Ortega took his time, even though he must have guessed the question was meant for him. He looked Dorne over coolly while he lit a cigarette in the Mexican manner—by holding its end to the flaring match.

"I can vouch for eet, señor," he spoke at last. "Thees whiskaired hombre pull the gon—whssst! An' call the Señor Mendota the bad name. W'ot would you? Don Pedro had no recourse except his gon, eef he would save hees life."

"Yeah," growled Dorne sceptically. "Happened just like it always has every time Mendota adds another notch to his hawg-laig."

He whirled at a soft chuckle behind him. Mendota stood there, between Dorne and Tranter and the Wineglass puncher. And it was Mendota who had chuckled. There was a feline grin still on his lips. He placed his glance on Dorne's face and held it there mockingly.

"What would you, señor?" he grinned, and shrugged, spreading out his long-fingered hands. "It ees the fate."

"Then yore fate better undergo a damn swift change," Dorne snapped. "Because the next time you're forced to kill a man I'm goin' to pistol-whip you outa town!"

Two days passed uneventfully, as they usually do in the south-west cattle country—save around places like Spavined Nag, where the isolated nature of the country attracts tough hombres with a craving for dodging necktie parties or long-term jails. But such apparent passiveness on the part of the hard cases composing the sporting element was certainly unusual there. It began to get on Dorne's nerves as no amount of hell-bending action could have. He was frankly worried, and said as much to Tranter as they met in the Sheriff's Office on the morning of the third day after Mendota's shooting scrap.

"Don't git roiled up about it," Tranter advised with characteristic imperturbability. "Ain't no use yore frettin'. Things'll be happenin' soon enough. You take it from a man what knows. Why," he ran a gnarled hand through the rumpled hair showing beneath his shoved-back hatbrim, "I recollect when I was down round the Pan-handle one year, I saw a sim'lar spell of sugar-coated calm. Boy, these calm spells is shore real trouble-breeders! This time, I recall, some gents was plannin' to rob the gold express. An' they shore did, too. Busted 'er plumb wide open an' made a fifty thousan' dollar haul! They—"

"What I'm interested in," cut in Dorne drily, "is who busted forty thousand outa the Stockman's

Bank of Spavined Nag! That's what I wanta hear about. Put your recollectin' energy to work on that an' we'll be gettin' someplace, mebbe."

"Yeah—mebbe," Tranter said, but did not display any great enthusiasm in the possibilities. "Tell yuh what I will do, though. Let's you an' me take another pasear over that there bank. Mebbe we overlooked somethin' the other time. Fella never knows. Now if we could get somethin' on one of these gunslammin' hellions round here it might give us the toe-holt we're a-needin'. I swear tuh Hannah, it sure looks like this yere bank-robber was one old hand at the game. I recollect the time Jesse James was a-tellin' me—"

"Tie up the little bull," Dorne said, "an let's get started. Not," he added, "that I got any hopes we'll find anythin'. But even movin' round is better'n settin' here."

"Yeah," Tranter mopped his beaded brow as he got to his feet, "this shore is the most thirstiest climate ever I see. Sun—sun—an' more sun; each minute hotter'n the next. Hell's hinges ain't got nothin' on Spavined Nag when it comes to downright heat an' general cussedness!"

"Save some of that wind to cool yore porridge," Bill Dorne snapped, irritated at the lack of progress they'd been making concerning the mystery of the looted bank. More than that in fact was bothering him. He could not understand Borst's unusual calm indifference to the insult of being run out of town by an old customer on whom the badge of authority had been pinned. He had been expecting swift reprisal. Yet, aside from Mendota's gunplay, Dorne could not see but what the town's sporting element was on the way to becoming right down docile. It wasn't natural! Then, too, he felt a vaguely restless itch to go out and see how Lola was making out.

He did not like to think of her working in Borst's wolf den. He'd expostulated with her no later than the other night. But to no avail. She'd only laughed, and assured him that she was very well able to take care of herself. He followed Tranter to the door, still engrossed in his milling thoughts. But once outside in the hot smash of the morning sun he took the lead, swinging out toward the bank with springy, jingling strides.

Fisk met them in the lobby. Bank business appeared to be going on about as usual. Save for the worried lines in Fisk's pale face, one would hardly have guessed that the Stockman's Bank had sustained a forty-thousand dollar loss.

Fisk greeted them with the question uppermost in his mind: "Have you caught the robber?"

"Hell, no," Tranter growled, before Bill could frame a proper reply. "We got tuh give the cuss a decent chance tuh spend the swag he's lifted, ain't we? What the hell kinda law officers would we be if we nabbed that misguided pilgrim before he had a chance tuh blow his loot?"

A man came in through the open door behind them as Fisk turned his scowl on Dorne. "Is that the attitude you're takin', Sheriff?" he demanded indignantly.

"No," Bill's tone was short. "We'll nab yore man. Just give us time—"

"That's right," the newcomer interrupted. "The ways of the Lord in Spavined Nag are not only inscrutable, but downright leisurely. The only thing that moves in a hurry round this sink of iniquity, this cesspool of immorality, this den of thieves and assassins, this—this—well, the only thing that raises dust is the Devil's business, which goes on every minute. What's to be done, I'd like to know, about the funds of the Lord which I deposited in this mismanaged institution?"

The banker's pallid countenance purpled. Tranter's jaw dropped open, then closed with a click of teeth. "By cripes, Reverend," he grunted admiringly, "yuh shore got the gift o' gab!"

Dorne turned to Gospel Jones politely. "How much had the Church on deposit here?" he asked, diffidently.

The sky-pilot of Spavined Nag grinned sheepishly. "Wal, Bill, you know the Devil's got a stranglehold on this here cowtown that's uncommon hard to break. The Lord didn't have but five measly dollars in this palace of the moneychangers."

"Shucks," Bill said, pulling a slender roll from his chaps pocket and peeling therefrom a ten-dollar banknote which he tendered to Gospel Jones. "Take this, Parson, an' give the Lord's funds a new lease on life."

"Wal, now that's what I call uncommon kind," said Jones heartily. "Bill, the Lord's grateful—almost as much as me, in fact. Strike me dead if the Lord's pickin's ain't almighty lean round this man's town, an' the doves which fetch the meat an' bread to His loyal followers has sure enough done got sidetracked in this thirstin' wilderness of onregenerated sin. I ain't et a decent meal in three days."

"Well, don't use that ten-spot tuh feed *yore* face," Tranter protested, hurriedly digging down into his own pocket. "It don't seem right that the Lord's funds should be used fer no such foolish purpose. If you got a itchin fer the nose-bag, take this quarter down to the Chink's an he'll fix you up some grub that'll take the wrinkles plumb outen yore belly. You better put that ten-spot in the bank fore she burns a hole in yore pocket—"

"The Lord turns the other cheek," Gospel Jones said knowingly, "but I ain't got to be that much of a Christian, yet, I reckon. I'll take this two-bits piece, Brother—an' thank you. But the Lord's funds'll be a dangsite safer in my pocket than in a bank what makes a specialty of extendin' a field of operations to the Philistines."

Banker Fisk's scowl followed him out the door. He muttered something under his breath that had the tone of being a trifle uncomplimentary. But Tranter could not quite make up his mind whether the remark had been addressed to the sky-pilot or the Sheriff's Office.

Fisk said, "Haven't you made any progress on this case at all?"

"Well, yeah," Bill replied sarcastically. "The Sheriff's Office has the case well in hand an' the public may expect an arrest at any moment."

"I don't consider this a proper subject for levity," Fisk grunted. "Things have been going from bad to worse—fast. An' your election to the badge-totin' fraternity ain't improved 'em enough to make a gnat's eye water."

"It ain't, eh?" Bill snapped, and returned the banker's scowl with interest. "Listen," he said; "listen—I'm the peacefullest jasper ever was foaled. When folks lets me have my way. But when gents gets to makin' the kinda remark *you* jest made, an' tries to order me round an' run my office, why I jest naturally cloud all up for a big rain. Fisk, you be careful or you're gonna get wet!"

And with an angry snort Bill Dorne started for the door.

But not so Buck Tranter. That ragged deputy—on whom, by his own word, you could smell the powder smoke—was lookin' at the banker's left coat pocket, which was hanging rather oddly as though some object, too big to fit, were leaning in it slantways.

"How long since you taken tuh totin' a knife round with yuh, Fisk?" he asked, with a saturnine eye on the banker's face. "Yuh must be dealin' with some pretty tough customers when yuh find it necessary tuh—"

"This knife," Fisk cut in, pulling the weapon gingerly from his coat pocket, "was in the safe. I—I was about to call Bill's attention to it when that Parson Jones sidetracked me." He held it out and Tranter took it promptly, lest he change his mind.

"In the safe, eh? Yuh mean, I reckon, in the vault that robber busted open."

"Yes," Fisk took off his glasses and polished them with a handkerchief taken from the left breast pocket of his coat. He peered through the glasses, then satisfied, put them back on and returned the handkerchief to his pocket, dropping in the process a tiny bit of paper. Which he failed to notice.

Tranter unostentatiously planted one big spurred boot upon it while saying, as he turned the Bowie over and over in his hands, "This here's right smart of a knife, Fisk. Reg'lar Arkansas toothpick. Whose do you suppose it is?"

"Don't know, I'm sure," said the banker testily. "How would *I* know? I just told you I picked it up off the floor of the vault."

"How d'you reckon it got there?" Tranter asked as, curious, Bill Dorne came back.

"I guess the robber must have dropped it."

"He sure picked a poor place," Tranter commented sardonically. "D'you know a feller name of Dode Harniss? He works with cows."

The banker's expression said he did not associate with persons who worked with cows. But aloud he said, "No," and let it go at that.

"Hmm." Tranter let his glance rove beyond Fisk's shoulder, suddenly let it widen, depicting startled incredulity. Moved by instinct, the banker whirled. As he did so Tranter stooped, scooped something from the floor beneath his boot and straightened. He was innocently paring his fingernails with the bowie knife when Fisk turned round again.

Fisk growled, "What were you looking at?"

"Me?" Tranter seemed amazed. "Nothin' as I knows of. Why?"

With an impatient snort the banker, muttering something about the banker's business having to go on, departed. Dorne and Tranter did likewise.

When they got back to the Sheriff's Office, Dorne said: "Well?"

"Dang right," Buck Tranter chuckled. "That vinegaroon claimed he picked this Arkansas toothpick off the floor o' that vault. Uncommon strange, says I. It wa'n't there when we went over the place two-three days ago! Where'd it come from? Bill, this thing's a snare an' a delusion—it's a plant!"

"What for?" Dorne's narrowed eyes were on Tranter closely. "Why should Fisk want to plant evidence in his own vault?"

"How should I know?" Tranter countered. "But I'm bettin' it's a plant though, jest the same. Anyhow, you know well as I do it wasn't there the other day."

"Whose is it? Do you recognize it?"

"This hawg-sticker," Tranter said impressively, "belonged to Dode Harniss the las' time I saw him, three-four years ago."

Dorne started. "You sure?"

"Plumb positive. I reckon I ort tuh know. He tried tuh lift my scalp with it over some skirt in Sante Fe!"

Dorne's face showed that he caught the significance of this. Dode Harniss was one of the two Wineglass punchers who had been riding circle on the night the rustlers lifted one-hundred-and-fifty prime two-year-olds from Mayor Globe's range—and since that night he had not been seen.

IX / "A DUDE JUST GOT KILLED"

"You mean—?" Dorne said, coldly drawling.

"I mean it looks tuh me like that smug pelican of a Chessycat-grinnin' Fisk is mixed up in this dang lootin' somehow, an' is tryin' tuh lay the blame onto Dode Harniss!" Tranter growled with emphasis.

"But why?"

"Don't ast me foolish questions," Tranter snapped. "I ain't no blinkin' mind-reader!"

"But didn't you tell me only yesterday that Dode Harniss was a tough hombre—plumb cultus, I believe you said?"

"An' what if I did? He shore was a ornery cuss when I knew him. What's that got tuh do with Fisk findin' his knife on the—"

Dorne interruped: "It mebbe has a-plenty to do with it, Buck. If Fisk found this Harniss' knife on the floor of the bank vault—"

"But," Tranter cut in swiftly, "*we* didn't find it there! An' we shore looked for it like a Scotchman what's dropped a penny. Leastways, we was lookin' for anything we could find, an' if it had been there we'd 'a' found it!"

"I reckon we would," Bill said thoughtfully.

"It sure looks like Banker Fisk is pullin' a fast one. An' speakin' of fast ones, Buck, I been hearin' that Borst is gettin' pretty gay out there at his new location. S'pose you fork yore bronc out there now an' serve warnin' on him. Tell him from me that if he don't tone down an' start runnin' a decent joint, I'm comin' out there an' bust his place to kindlin' wood."

Reluctantly, Tranter got up and sauntered out of the door. It was hot outside—hotter than blue blazes—and Dorne didn't much blame the ragged deputy for not wanting to take a three-mile ride. But somebody had to do it. Borst must be kept in hand, he told himself. For Borst was one of those gents that take a mile every time you allow them an inch.

Left to himself, Dorne put his time to good use. He lined things up for review across the screen of his mind. This bank robbery business was beginning to assume unexpected proportions. Imagine Fisk pulling a stunt like that. Why, he must have robbed his own bank! Anyway, he very evidently had had a hand in the robbing, and was—"Ah!" Bill growled. "I'm bettin' he hired Harniss to pull that lootin'. An' now that it's over Fisk is figurin' to deal himself the pot by framin' up on Harniss. Ain't no other way he could of got Dode's knife, less'n Dode was 'sociatin' with him."

But as he thought it over, Bill came to the conclusion that this theory was anything but waterproof. He found hole after hole to his chain of reasoning. Disgruntled, he got to his feet and paced the floor, hands deep-thrust in his chaps pockets.

Another notion came to him regarding the means by which Harniss' knife might have come into Fisk's possession. After all, he mused, they did not know that Harniss had joined the rustlers who had raided the Wineglass range the other night. Actually, he and his pardner, Ed Krayson, might have been captured somehow by the cattle thieves and, for some ulterior purpose not to be found by surface indications, forced to go with the rustlers and their stolen stock. Yet even so, if Fisk were honest, Dorne could not see how he had come by Harniss' knife.

But assume for the moment that Fisk *was* crooked, and things straightened themselves out beautifully. If the rustlers had taken the two Wineglass punchers captive, Fisk might have come into possession of that Arkansas tickler through his association with the man or men behind these rustling activities. And Bill would have bet his last shirt that man was Borst!

But there were still plenty of loopholes in his reasoning, as he was forced to admit. Ed Krayson and Harniss *might* have *somehow* been captured by the rustlers, but to Dorne this seemed mighty unlikely. And even so, what possible motive could the rustlers have had for forcing the two punchers into accompanying them? It would have been much more in character for the cattle thieves to have shot the Wineglass circle riders out of hand. And Dorne knew it.

Furthermore, assuming that Fisk *was* guilty of robbing his own bank (and this was a possibility that clung tenaciously to Bill's thoughts), why should he affiliate himself with the sporting crowd, thus forcing himself to share the proceeds of his own villainy? It didn't make sense—unless, and Bill's brow darkened, that sanctimonious old smug-face, Fisk, had been dealing from a crooked deck right straight along. In which case it would be natural for him and Borst to have an understanding. Crooks didn't operate around Spavined Nag without splitting their swag with Borst!

Somehow, the mutations of Bill Dorne's wandering thoughts swung abruptly to Tumbleweed, the undercover deputy. Perhaps it was the association of ideas. But, anyway, his thoughts went now to his newest deputy. What was the fellow doing? Had he uncovered anything of import? Why hadn't he got some message to Bill as to his progress and present whereabouts?

Questions, questions, and *more* questions! But no answers. Dorne scowled. There was something about that Tumbleweed gent . . . He shook his head and turned his attention to Polsky, Globe's Wineglass foreman. An odd stick. Close-mouthed as the proverbial clam. And handy with his hog-leg—uncommon handy for a peaceable, run-of-the-range ramrod. There were lots of things about "Hoot Owl" Polsky—so-called because of the extremely sober cast of his countenance—that Dorne would have given the loose change that clinked in his pocket to know.

Polsky had arrived one day some eight months past, and had been promptly hired by Globe as foreman. Why? The man knew cows—no question about that. He knew how to run a big spread, too. And appeared aware of the frailties of human nature. But how had Globe known this when hiring the fellow? What sort of credentials had Hoot Owl shown? How had he happened to hit Globe for the job in the first place? Globe hadn't been short-handed at the time; in fact he had fired his top screw without notice to make a place for Polsky. Dorne had often wondered about that. It looked almost as though the two—Globe and Polsky—were old acquaintances.

Dorne thought briefly of Marcia and determined sheepishly that it was about time for him to be stopping by the Mayor's place. He hadn't been there since the late afternoon of the night the bank had been robbed. He guessed an engaged fellow had ought to be a bit more attentive. Resolving to drop by and "visit a spell" with Marcia before the day was out, he turned his mind to other things—the jingling clump of booted feet now approaching along the plank sidewalk outside.

He nodded as Tranter stepped into the office.

"You made good time," he commented, and got out his pipe and packed it. "How'd he take it?"

"Didn't see 'im," Tranter sighed, and mopped the perspiration from his forehead. "That Gleed fella told me Borst wasn't around. Said he'd gone out to the ranch. Does he own a spread sure enough? Or was that jest a gag tuh git me on m' way?"

"He owns one," Dorne admitted. "Good one, too. The Hashknife. Over in Gypsum Valley—which ain't as dry as it sounds. What did Gleed have to say about my orders?"

"Not s'much as I figgered he would," Tranter answered dolefully. "Fer a minute he sorta clouded up an' I was hopin fer the best. Then he seemed tuh reelect that he was talkin' tuh ol' He-Man Tranter's li'l son Buck—same being a holster-hopper on which the brimstone shore does linger. He backed off then, like he wasn't wantin' no part in what I reckon he c'd see I was honin' tuh give 'im. He nods his bullet head an' says as how he'll pass the word tuh the Boss. But, yuh know, Bill—I got a sneakin' idee that Borst was right there in that back room. I c'd hear voices. Couldn't make out nothin', but one of them warbles shore sounded like Borst's cooin' purr."

Dorne weighed this, then nodded. And his eyes were a deeper blue, it looked to Tranter. Dorne said, "Didn't see Tumbleweed round there anyplace, did you?"

"Wal, now that's a funny thing, Bill. But since yuh mentioned it—yeah. I seen him, but he seen me first—an' cleared out like he had urgent business elsewhere."

"Didn't see where he went, did you?"

"He went waltzin' right intuh that back room. Where I heard the voices," Tranter grunted, and scowled. "If yuh'd 'a' taken the advice of a man what knows, yuh'd never made that leather-faced hyena no propersishun. He'll make yuh rue the day yuh took up with him yet—yuh wait an' see. He's got a eye what's meaner'n gar soup. A killer eye, that's what he's got. An' don't say I didn't warn yuh, when yore friends is packin' yuh slow an' mournful-like towards Boot Hill."

Bill snorted. "Yuh can leave that crepe with Borst. Tell me, did you see that Lola girl?"

"I'd think yore mind would be occypied with that Marcia gal right now," said Tranter drily. "I'm tellin' yuh. This two-gal business don't never work out tuh no good end. Yuh'll hev each of them feemales a-thinkin' yo're sweetest on the other, an' there'll be hair flyin' shore, if yuh don't cut it out. One string's enough for yore bow at a time, son. Take it from a man what knows.

"I been around a fortnight or two. An' I've met women—plenty of 'em. Taken by an' large, they're the salt of the earth. But take 'em two at a time, an' hell beside 'em would be a quiet place! Anyhow, yuh've gone an' got yoreself engaged tuh marry the Mayor's daughter. Yuh better steer plumb clear of that Lola skirt. Onless yo're courtin' ol' man Globe with a shotgun."

Bill flushed, and being aware of the fact—and of Tranter's twinkling regard—scowled savagely.

"Borst's place," Tranter added, before Bill could frame a scorching reply, "has done got itself a new monicker. The Three-Mile House they calls it now. An' there's a dude out there what somebody orta keep his eye on. My Gawd, but that fella's green. Got money in every pocket. Hard money, too, judgin' by the jingle. Talk about your lamb in the wolf's den. Boy, ef Borst don't hang him out tuh dry, my name ain't Buck Tranter!"

"What's he doin' out there?"

"I ast him. He allows he come in on the stage this mawnin', an' seein' some of Borst's hangers-on lollin' round them outbuildin's, figgers he'd hit town, an' he got off. Time he'd realized his mistake, the stage was halfway tuh town. But accordin' tuh what I could hear, they been entertainin' him right royal. I tried tuh wise 'im up. But he tells me real indignant like, tuh mind m' own business an' re—*refrain* from callin' his friends op—opprobious ethipets. Cripes!" Tranter snorted, "he's prime fer a pluckin'—*an' he'll get one, too!*"

"Oh, I dunno," countered Bill. "You carried my message to them warnin' 'em to tread easy for a spell. I don't think they'll bother that dude overmuch. Might part him from some of this loose cash. But I don't reckon they'll roll him, or anything like that."

"Live an' learn," grunted Tranter, shaking his head. "There ain't no fool like a young 'un."

Bill Dorne grinned. "Cheer up, you ol' damp covering; times are gettin' better."

"Yeah?" said Tranter sceptically. "Wal, how about advancin' me somethin' tuh smoke, ag'in my wages? I done chawed m' Brown's Mule plumb up entire. That there pipe yo're smokin' has a real lively smell. Ef yuh've got any more terbaccy like what yo're smokin', I wouldn't mind rollin' me a quirley."

Bill tossed his sack over and watched Tranter's knobby fingers expertly twist a pinch of tobacco and a brown rice paper into a perfectly smooth round cylinder. Lighting his smoke, Tranter calmly dropped the sack in his pocket, and changed the subject.

Squinting his eyes to keep the spiralling smoke out, he spread a crumpled scrap of paper on one corduroyed knee and smoothed it out. "This here," he grunted softly, "is what I picked up over to the bank. It dropped outa Fisk's coat pocket when he was gettin' out a nose rag tuh wipe his specs. I got a hunch he's gonna be some perturbed when he finds he's lost it. Yuh might look it over," he added, and held it out to Dorne.

Bill took it, and the following instant let out a

startled oath. His cheeks were taut and his wide lips grim as he read for the second time:

"Three-Mile House Wednesday night at 11:45."

There was no greeting and no signature; just those six words and four numbers—but Banker Fisk had been carrying the paper in his pocket. And the Three-Mile House was the name of Borst's new resort. The inference was obvious. Bill swore.

"Were you out to Borst's place last night?"

"Yeah," said Tranter. "But later—must have been round one o'clock."

"Didn't see Fisk?"

"He ain't exactly crazy, is he?"

"Well—skip it, then. Did you see Borst?"

Tranter nodded. "He looked like the cat that licked the cream. He," the ragged deputy chuckled, "give me a ceegar!"

"Must have been feelin' pretty chipper," Bill growled viciously.

"That's what I thought," Tranter said, and sobered. "Now look, Bill—S'posin' some of Borst's hands ran off them Wineglass critters th' other night. An' s'posin, them two circle riders of Globe's threw in with 'em. Then—"

"That don't take a whale of a lot of supposin'," Bill grunted testily.

"Nope," Tranter said, "it don't. Then supposin'

that much is true. What would *you* do in Borst's place, was you as ornery an' greedy as he is? . . . Wait—lemme tell yuh! You'd likely put them two hombres outa their misery once their use was over. Then, tuh make sure folks wasn't suspectin' you or any of yore gang of robbin' the Stockman's Bank, it would come in right handy to plant that knife of Harniss' on the scene of the lootin'. *That,*" he concluded triumphantly, "is what that note was sent Fisk for, I'm bettin'. Borst got him out there, give him the knife an' told him tuh plant it. Only trouble was, we seen Fisk before he'd had a chance tuh cache it."

"Or," said Bill, thoughtfully nodding, "knowin' we'd been over the place pretty thoroughly, Fisk hadn't figured out a safe place to put it where 'twould be effective, an' still not give his hand away. Buck, I believe you've got somethin' there."

Tranter, about to add something to the conversation, abruptly shut his mouth and turned as fast-drumming hoofs beat down the dusty street. Both he and Dorne made for the door to see what was up. Dorne reached it first and pushed outside into the broiling glare of the nooning sun. A horse and rider were spurring down the main street as though the Devil was reaching for the mustang's broomtail.

Straight up to the Sheriff's Office the clattering rider thundered, hitting dirt on braking bootheels as he threw his pony back on its haunches in a slithering stop. He was a puncher from one of the outlying ranches, Bill thought, vaguely remembering having seen the fellow's face before.

"What's up?" Bill demanded tensely.

"Hell's crick!" the puncher gasped. "A dude just got killed at the Three-Mile House!"

X / HEAVY, HEAVY—

"What's that?" Bill grabbed the fellow by the shoulders. *"Who got killed?"*

"That dang dude what was throwin' his dinero right an' left out to Borst's new joint."

"Who killed him?" Bill drawled, dangerously soft.

"Cock Robin," Tranter interjected. "I told yuh somethin' would happen tuh that jigger! Never let it be said I didn't warn yuh!"

Bill paid Tranter no attention. "Who killed him?" he repeated ominously.

"Damfino! Fella called Tumbleweed gave me half a dollar to ride in an' wise yuh up to the killin'. All I know is what he tol' me. I was playin' poker. All of a sudden, I heard a shot in that back room. I started for the outside door pronto. An' just as I got to m' hawss, up comes this fella who gives his name as Tumbleweed an' says, 'Ride in an' tell the Sheriff that dude's been shot!'"

"How long ago was this?"

"Not twenty minutes."

Bill said, "Get our hawsses, Buck. An' don't stop to pick no daisies." Still looking at the messenger, he added musingly, "Don't I know you? Seems like we've met up before someplace." He saw a film of caution spread across the other's eyes. But the man's expression did not change.

"You might know me," he admitted. "I been around this part of the country quite a spell. Been workin' for Ol' Man Hartley over on the north side of the Blue Range. Wagonwheel. Reckon I better be siftin' along now I—"

"How'd you happen to be out at Borst's?" Bill asked.

"I come in fer the mail. Stopped off at this Three-Mile House tuh wet m' whistle," the fellow said, reasonable enough. Yet somehow, Bill had a notion that the man was lying. Tranter arrived with their horses just then, however, effectively preventing him from questioning the puncher further. "Drop in again next time you're in town," he said. "We'll talk this over again. I'd like to get a line on that Tumbleweed fella."

The puncher nodded. "Okay, Sheriff. Be seein' yuh," and off he went with a wave of the hand.

Bill climbed into the saddle. "Seems like I've seen that fella someplace, Buck," he said. "But I'll be danged if I can place him."

"Wal, I don't know him from Adam's off-ox," Tranter said. "Let's go."

Inside the bar-room of the Three-Mile House, Borst eyed his two chief gunslammers grimly. A dead quiet obtained within the place, although beyond the batwing doors the yard outside seemed astir with a methodical activity.

Borst said quietly, "Bill Dorne an' that ragbag

deputy of his will be out here in about three shakes. Bill's got an undercover man workin' here an' I jest seen him pass a tip to a puncher about that damn nosey dude we jest gave a ticket to the Great Beyond."

The gunmen's eyes glistened at these words. Then—

"Mebbe—" Joe Fuddabaugh began, when Borst cut him off. "They'll be here, all right, an' you can bank on that. We're gonna beat Bill, but he won't take it layin' down. Remember," he paused to be certain he had their full attention; "remember that when they get here I'm countin' on you boys to earn yore keep. An' there'll be two hundred apiece in it for you if you don't gum the works. I don't want to slip-up. Bill Dorne's dynamite, in case you don't know. Get him first pop or you won't get him at all. I ain't real sure about that deputy, but you better get him, too. Wait till they shove in these swingin' doors, then give 'em all you got. An' that won't be too much. I want Bill stopped definite, once an' for all—plumb final!"

"But," Smoky Leupp, the second of Borst's pair of ace gundogs, protested. "Supposin' the undercover squirt yuh mentioned cuts in or spills the play?"

"He won't," Borst assured them with a wolfish grin. "I'm keepin' him busy someplace else. . . . Lola. You can forget him entirely. Jest keep yore minds fixed on rubbin' out Bill Dorne. That's all you got to do, an' I'll be takin' care of anythin' else that comes up. Get set now—here they come!"

Putting their broncs over the ground at a hard gallop, it was not long before Bill Dorne and the ragged Tranter neared Borst's new Three-Mile House. Looking toward it, where it lay sweltering in the sun's noontime blaze, Bill reflected that there was a look about the place that went uncommon well with murder.

He and Tranter swung lightly from their saddles before the hitch rail fronting the main building, ground-tied their mustangs and started for the newly-installed batwing doors.

Several men, working about the pole corral a short distance off, looked up curiously. But said nothing. Neither did Bill or Tranter—to them. To Bill, Tranter said, "Don't it never rain in this yere country? Cripes, I'm thirsty enough tuh put down ever' last bottle behind Borst's bar."

"Borst's bar," Bill told him grimly, "ain't goin' to be fit for nothin' but kindlin' when we walk out of this joint, Buck. He's gettin' plumb outa the resort business here an' now—plumb complete. I've warned him twice; this is the time I act! When I say a thing I mean it!"

"Seems like if yuh was fixin' tuh start a corpse-an'-cartridge occasion out yere," Tranter muttered, "yuh'd oughta brung a posse. We're goin' tuh be outnumbered six or eight tuh one. Them there's pretty powerful long odds, ef anyone sh'd ride up an' ask yuh."

"If you're scared," Bill drawled scathingly, "yuh can climb back into yore saddle an' start throwin' dust."

"Scared! Who? *Me?*" Tranter loosed a flood of educating profanity. "Why, dang yore everlastin' tintype! How'n seventeen prairie chickens do yuh make that out? I'll have yuh know a Tranter never backed down from anythin'—not even the flood! Scared—hell! Bring on yore durn lead-throwers; I'll show yuh how we washes 'em up back in Texas!" And the scowl that furrowed his countenance and the blaze in his squinted eyes told Bill that there was no fear in the lanky deputy.

"I was just joshin'," he soothed, and added: "Sure hope Mendota's here. I'm pinin' to ask him what he done the other day to make that fool desert rat drag a gun. He mebbe drawed first, like Mendota an' Ortega claimed, but I'm bettin' Mendota egged the old coot into it."

"Wal, here we are," Tranter said. "Who goes in first—the Sheriff or his deputy?"

XI / "FILL YORE HAND"

"The Sheriff," Bill said, as they paused before the steps. "But he ain't goin' in like no bull through a Chink shop, an' you can stick yore pin in that!" Dropping his voice and letting his words come from between lips that hardly moved, he added, "No sense in us takin' extra chances. A ounce of prevention is worth a pound of cure—that's a ol' Dorne sayin', Buck, an' we're gonna 'bide by it. You sneak round to the back door; you'll find one round there someplace. You slip in, an' when you're set say somethin' loud enough so's I can hear it. This may not be no trap, but I ain't figurin' to put m' foot in it just to have the satisfaction of findin' out—"

"I ain't a heap partial tuh puttin' my hoof in it neither," Tranter objected. "But I'll do it, bein' it's you what's askin'." And, spitting on his badge and polishing it with his sleeve, Tranter went striding round toward the rear of the Three-Mile House.

Bill bent down and pretended to be adjusting a spur while he waited for Tranter's signal. Out of the corner of his eyes he slantwise watched the group loafing about the new corral. They seemed to be paying no special attention to either him or the vanished Tranter. He was beginning to get a crick in his back from his bent posture when at last he caught Tranter's booming voice.

"Wal, suff'rin' sidewinders, Sheriff,' he said, "fancy meetin' *you* here!"

Straightening, Dorne pushed through the swinging doors into a room filled with a tight, electric silence—a room wherein Borst's chief pair of gunslammers were poised, one to either side of the batwings, in a coiled crouch with their hands gripping guns and their guns pointed toward the entrance. But Tranter was behind them, as they well knew without having to look, and they dared not move from their tracks.

Dorne streaked a grin. "Playin' a new game, gents?" he greeted the glowering gun fighters. "Or is it ring-around-the-rosy?"

Joe Fuddabaugh swore. But his pardner only glared murderously and his fingers tightened on his gun as though he were of half a mind to bring its muzzle up and use it. But he stiffened when Tranter from his easy slouch beside the bar said, suggestively:

"That bet yuh had with me, Bill, about pickin' off ears at twenty paces, still hold good? These here fellas would be jest about right, I'm thinkin'. That Leupp jasper has ears like a giraffe, an' his companero has the same kinda pointed fuzzy ones that usual grow on jackasses. I don't reckon neither would miss 'em a heap was I tuh shoot 'em off."

This time it was Smoky Leupp who swore. And he did so viciously. "You better laugh while you got the chance, you addlebrained nitwit, because once you lose that drop I'm gonna perforate yuh like a sieve!"

"Shucks," Tranter said, "I ain't even got my gun out. What's the matter with you rim-fire dally men?"

"They ain't got no sand in their craws when a gent's lookin' at 'em, Buck," Dorne depreciated. But he watched them closely. "They're the brave kinda tinhorns what only plays with stacked decks. I wouldn't be surprised if they was layin' for some poor misguided pilgrim when we came in. Like that dude they jest bumped off—"

"That's a lie," snarled Smoky Leupp. "I never even seen the dude!"

"You'll never be able to make a jury swaller that," Dorne said. And Tranter added, comfortingly, "Not that it'll ever git to a jury."

Leupp made his play then, frightened by the shadow of the noose. And Joe Fuddabaugh was quick to back him up. Smoky even got in first shot. But it buried its bullet harmlessly into the floor, three feet in front of Dorne.

Dorne was firing from the hip, and driving each shot with a wicked coldness that could have but one end—and had it. Smoky Leupp was dead when he struck the floor.

Joe Fuddabaugh fared better. But not much. He had whirled, bringing his pistol upward in a swing for the third button of Tranter's shirt. But Tranter broke both his arms at the elbow before he could squeeze the trigger. Then, with professional indifference, Tranter sent in two more shots that knocked Joe's legs from under him and dropped him, a moaning heap of misery, not two feet from where his pardner lay in a motionless huddle.

"You was a little hasty Bill," Tranter commented judiciously. "We don't kill 'em down in Texas—we jest cripples 'em up fer life as a object lesson to others of their ilk." He grinned, then adding:

"Statistics proves it works out better thataway. Texas ain't got no ring-tailed hellions anymore, except what's too crippled to practise—the rest has all moved into Arizony."

Bill could hear the pound of running feet now as men converged excitedly upon the place to see what had happened—probably, he thought, to look with satisfaction upon his and Tranter's corpses. They were due for quite a shock, he reflected sardonically, and turned to face the batwings.

But it was not from the front entrance that visitors of import came. He swung round again as Tranter said, "Afternoon, Mr. Borst. Nice day for thirsty weather. How 'bout settin' 'em up on the house? These corpse-an'-cartridge episodes allus make me thirsty 'nuff tuh drink the Injun Ocean."

"What the hell you birds been up to?" Borst exploded as Bill faced him.

"Oh," said Bill, "we just been givin' a coupla

sidewindin' killers their marchin' orders. One of 'em's marched his last, an' the other 'un's goin' to do the rest of his marchin' on crutches. *Know 'em?*" he snapped the last two words at Borst like the crack of a whip.

But Borst had himself in hand. His face did not shed its expression of indignant horror by so much as a fraction. "You can't get away with this," he growled. "This town's had all the legal homicides it's goin' to, if I got anythin' to say about it. I'll have your badges before the sun sets."

"Yeah? You an' who else?" sneered Tranter.

Dorne said, before Borst could round up a suitable reply, "Do you know these hombres?" and the gun that still was in his hand made a brief gesture to the two luckless gunmen prostrated on the sawdust floor.

"No, I don't know 'em," Borst snarled. "D'you think I keep tabs on all the riff-raff that use my place to loaf in? You can't talk to me like this, Bill Dorne! There's a law in this country an'—"

"Don't make me laff," Bill drawled. Backing closer to the bar so that he could keep his eyes on Borst and the group of men standing huddled between the batwings, he flung out his order tersely:

"I want every man an' woman cleared out of this buildin' pronto. Get 'em out, Borst."

"I'll be damned if I will! You ain't runnin' my place! You ain't—"

"Save a part of yore breath for breathin'," Dorne advised. "You're listenin' to the voice of authority, Mister. Get busy!"

"You can't—" Borst began again.

"Listen," Bill said flatly, and there was that in his tone that showed he would take no more lip from any man. "Before you get shut of me you're goin' to find out that there's a powerful lot of things that I can do. The word *can't* ain't in my dickshonary. Are you gonna clear them yaps outa here, or shall I do it?"

"Vamoose," Borst said, with a smothered oath, to the men who filled the doorways. "You heard the Sheriff orate. Must think he's Gawd A'mighty. But you better do like he says. It don't pay to argue," he added sneeringly, "with the man that's got the drop."

Like a flash Bill's gun was back in leather. "I don't need no drop when I'm bent on herdin' polecats. Anyone in them back rooms, Borst? If there is, get 'em out!"

"What's the big idea?" Borst asked, curious despite himself.

"I allow you'll be findin' out before a powerful great while shags along. Got an axe around here anyplace?"

"Might be one out in the cookshack—"

"Get it, Buck."

From where he stood, Bill caught sight then of Tumbleweed and Lola eyeing him curiously from outside through one of the open windows. But he gave no sign of being aware of their presence, and not for a moment did he turn his shoulders away from Borst's big rocklike figure.

"Get it, Buck," he said, and heard Tranter drag his spurs toward the rear door. "Watch out for trouble," he added softly. "If one of those hyenas out there bats an eye, don't argue—put a quick window in his skull."

"You're hellbent on pilin' up a lot to answer for, Bill Dorne," Borst said, and his thick lips tightened ominously. "An' you'll answer for it, too! You're cock of the walk right now, but how long will it last? A man's luck, Bill, is a fickle thing. You better take it easy. What do you think you're figurin' to do with that axe?"

"The answer to that," Bill grinned, "is goin' to cost you money, Borst. Good money. An' a lot of it."

Borst sneered, "Bah! Pride goes before a fall—an' you've sure got pride by the horns."

"If you feel lucky, fill yore hand."

"I'll wait," Borst muttered, and his high blood laid a definite flush across his beefy cheeks. A wicked restlessness seemed to be tugging at his lips, and it narrowed down his sleepy lids, hooding his eyes like a mask. But the hand that removed a cigar from his coat pocket and put it between his teeth was steady, and so was the hand with which he lit it. "I'll wait," he repeated, and filled his lungs with expensive smoke.

"You always was a good waiter," Bill jeered heavily.

"Yeah. An' I'll still be waitin' round this one-hawss town long after you been planted."

"Waitin' for more suckers like that dude, I guess."

"That's it."

Tranter came in with the axe and looked enquiringly at Dorne. So did Borst turn his regard that way. But it wasn't enquiring; it was expressionless as the unblinking eyes of a snake.

Bill said, "Wreck that bar."—Like that.

Borst let out an oath, and there was a wicked viciousness in his tone. "By Gawd, you can't cut it, Bill—!"

"Watch me. Go on, Buck—I wanta see some kindlin'. Quick."

XII / "CARRIED OUT FEET FIRST"

There was one long instant of total silence inside that room; a hush peopled with unuttered thoughts. A stillness that brought lines of strain upon the faces of those gaping watchers who stood peering in from beyond the windows. Then Tranter, gripping his rusty axe with grim right hand, started for the bar.

Even now Borst did not let his temper rush him; did not let it push him into a situation from which he might have found it necessary to retreat. It was worth something to Dorne to see him standing there, face bloated and purple from the spur of rage, yet raising not a finger as Tranter brought his axe up in an easy lift.

Borst's desire to come to physical grips with Dorne showed in his tautened cheeks like letters of fire. But he held his rage with an iron hand. This, his actions said, was not the time to stage reprisals—but the time would come! The look he drove at Dorne said that nothing could hold Pecos Borst back; that nothing ever had and nothing ever would!

And all this time Tranter was working with a will, a wide tight grin framing his yellowed teeth. The muscles bulged beneath his shirt each time he brought his rusty weapon down. He was wasting neither time nor strokes. Every downward swing was being made to count.

Dorne watched Borst with a steel-cold attention, yet he stood in an easy hipshot slouch that robbed his pose of menace—or added to that menace, according to the angle a man was viewing it from. Menacing or not, it kept Borst's hands away from his hips; kept them out of his pockets, too, and away from his sweaty armpits.

Yet maybe it wasn't Dorne's pose that kept Borst's position static. Perhaps it was something the big saloonman read in Dorne's blue glance. Or the cold grin that curled Dorne's saturnine lips.

Dorne said wickedly, "Like a picture from Carry Nation."

"It's a picture," Borst gritted, "I'm goin' to be a long time forgettin'."

"I'd bet on that," Dorne grinned back. Then to Tranter, "That'll be enough, now, Buck. Don't want you to wear yorese'f down to a shadow. Hold off awhile; there's other things to be done."

He flashed another look at Borst. "Got everyone outa here? Upstairs? Back rooms?" And, at Borst's sullen nod, "Well, if you ain't it's just their hard luck an' I ain't goin' to shed no tears about no cremated trash like the kind what runs in yore pack."

Borst's face showed a tinge of grey as some of its lively red washed out. "What's that?" The words come from him hoarse, gruff. *"Cremate?"*

"That's what I said. Ain't nothin' wrong with yore hearin', is there?" Dorne's mocking laugh cut across the stillness. "Ain't you grabbed holt of the idee yet? I'm goin' to burn this damn joint down."

Borst whispered, "You—you—"

"Outside!" Dorne snapped, and drew his gun from its holster.

For an instant then, it seemed that Borst would grab for his pistol anyway. The man looked on the ragged edge of murder, and his frame was shaking as though with ague. His mouth hung slack, and it seemed as though his eyes would burst from his apoplectic face.

"Look out," Tranter jeered, "yuh'll git a stroke."

Dorne motioned with his pistol toward the door. And Borst moved toward it as if filled with Jamaica rum, his gait almost a wooden stagger. He paused once and slowly turned his head toward Bill. A streak of rashness threw a fleeting shadow across his drawn and paling cheeks. Then it was gone and, with a tightening of his jaw, he strode outside.

"Bill," said Tranter, when once again they were comfortably ensconced in the Sheriff's Office in Spavined Nag, and the sun was drifting down behind the mountains to the west, "you've got more durned nerve'n a brass monkey!"

Dorne's lips streaked a smile as he rolled a cigarette.

"More nerve than sense," continued Tranter, warming up to his subject like a cat beneath a stove. "By Cripes, I dang near bust when yuh tol' Borst yuh was sorry the rest of his powder-an-ball men weren't round so's they could enjoy the moral o' what yuh was doin' as much as he was enjoyin' it! When he seen his place goin' up in smoke he was mad enough tuh chaw railroad spikes! Just what would yuh 'a' done if he'd called yore bluff? That's what I'd admire tuh know."

"I wasn't bluffin'," Dorne said shortly.

"Yeah—an' he wa'n't callin' none, neither! But you ain't kiddin' no ranny what's been around like I hev. If he *had* 'a' called yore bluff—"

Dorne said, "He didn't. Best let it go like that. Sufficient the time to the evil thereof. That's one of my mottoes. Another is, never trouble trouble till trouble troubles you. Abide by the Golden Rule, Buck, an' give all men a even break. Live in peace an' love yore neighbours an'—"

"I can see," Tranter snorted, fishing a battered and evil-smelling pipe from his trousers pocket, "that you've done got religion. You been listenin' tuh that sky-pilot till yuh're gettin' tuh palaver jest like 'im. You know dang well yuh can't live in peace an' amity with Brother Borst—not after what yuh done tuh him this afternoon. Cripes, he was plumb frothin' at the mouth when we cleared outa there. An' he'll keep right on a-frothin' till he evens up the score!"

"What a little ray of sunshine you turned out to be."

"Sunshine, hell!" Tranter snorted. "I believe in lookin' facts square in the eye!"

An apparently unbreakable serenity was observable now in Bill's blue glance. It made Tranter fidgety. It appeared to him that Dorne was all puffed up with his success. He didn't feel so optimistic himself. "Listen," he said. "That Borst hellion ain't gonna git no kind of rest till he's put his heel on yore neck. Depend upon it. That fella means bizness—I seen blood in his eye when he looked at you."

Spur chains jingled to the clump of booted feet without. A moment later a tall lean shadow darkened the doorway and Parson Jones followed it into the room. "Brother," he said solemnly, fixing Bill with a serious glance, "constant exposure to dangers lendeth contempt for them."

Dorne grinned. "I got an answer for that one. It's a heck of a lot healthier to meet danger than to wait for it. One of my mottoes," he added modestly.

"There's no fool like a young'un," Tranter said, and lit his pipe. "I been tryin' tuh tell him, but he knows it all. They ain't no use in arguin' with 'im, Parson. His head's got so big now he'll hev tuh git a new hat."

"What's the matter with you rannies?" Dorne asked, grinning. "I don't need no nurses."

"Not yet, mebbe," Tranter muttered testily.

"Borst ain't goin' to take that sittin' down, son,"

Parson Jones opined. "You better not hang around lighted places after dark. Nor ride along high ridges when you take yore horse for an airin'."

"Is that," Dorne asked, "general advice, or somethin' special?"

Jones said, "I ain't a fella to talk just to hear my teeth rattle."

"An' a wink's as good as a nod to a blind mule," Tranter added, disgustedly. "Parson, yuh're wastin' yore breath."

"What is this anyway? A wake?"

"There's talk goin' round this town," Jones said darkly.

"What kinda talk?"

"Just talk, son," the sky-pilot answered cautiously. "Things are bein' said, an' a number of hard cases has got their heads together. They seen that fire in town here. An' yore movements are the subject of considerable int'rest."

Dorne said, "Such popularity must be deserved," and his rash grin played across his lips.

"Listen," Jones said grimly. "Did you tell Borst to head for the tall tules?"

"I told him to hunt a hole, crawl in an' pull it in after him," Dorne answered. "I told him if I caught him runnin' another dive in this county, it would be the last one he ever ran anyplace."

"An' I expect quite a passle of hombres heard you?"

"They sure did if they was list'nin'."

"Don't you know that puts it up to Borst to make good? If he don't plant you now, he'll be laffed clean outa the county," Jones told him seriously.

"I want him out of the county," Dorne announced flatly. "I told him three days ago right here in town. An' he'll go under his own motion or he'll be carried out feet first. I aim to make this county, *an' this town,* fit places for people to live in."

"Well," Jones admitted, looking from Dorne to Tranter and back again, "a polecat like Pecos Borst *does* contaminate God's good scenery. But—I'm allowin' you've bit off more than you can chew, son. You ain't goin' to be able to enlist much help in a fight against Borst's crowd. They're too powerful. Least ways, for the married gents to buck. And the single fellows . . . Well, the unmarried boys are too hell-bent on havin' a good time to want to see you close things down. I admire yore spirit, but—"

"Fine, Parson," Dorne grinned. "I'm sure glad to hear you say it. Let's all go get a drink."

They went to Venta's place, the Broken Harp. Dorne vetoed Tranter's suggestion that they go to Ortega's Black Bottle Bar. He was still thinking about the desert rat killed by Mendota there, and how Ortega had sworn the sagebrusher was first to yank a gun.

Venta was behind the bar when they entered. He

greeted them with an oily smile. "Name yore poison, gents. The treat is on the house."

The three gave their orders and, when filled glasses were slid before them, Tranter said, "To the rubbin' out of Pecos Borst. Drink hearty, gents—an' you, too, Venta."

The drinks were downed. Venta beamed and his oily smirk reached nearly from ear to ear. "That Borst ain't helpin' my business any," he growled loudly. "I'll be glad to see the last of 'im."

"You have," Dorne told him calmly. "He's plumb washed up in this county. He'll be clearin' out, I reckon, soon's he can sell his spread."

Dorne bought a bottle then and the three of them adjourned to a table in the rear. Staring down into his drink with a morose eye, Parson Jones reflected, "Somethin' tells me this thing ain't over yet. Borst's takin' this too calm. Dorne, there's blood on the moon these days. I hate to say it, but I've got a hunch there's goin' to be some more killin' round here before we git a ordinance perhibitin' the carryin' of lethal weapons. They're still goin' strapped to every man's hip, an' when a man's got a thing, he usually likes to use it."

"Wonder if Borst got that dude's roll?" Tranter said.

Bill suggested that if he hadn't got it before killing him, he most certainly had got it afterward. Wasn't that what they'd killed him for?

Here Jones interrupted with an unexpected revelation. "No," he said, "I don't reckon it was. That dude was a Cattlemen's Association man. An' it's my guess Borst knew it."

Here, Dorne mused, was food for thought, and put his notion to the test.

If the dude, as Jones said, really was an agent of the Cattlemen's Association, it meant that the Association kind of thought that Borst might be mixed up in the wholesale rustling activities going on in the locality. Spavined Nag and the surrounding range was putting on its war paint for rustlers, looked like. Honest ranchers would soon be coming into town with blood in their eyes and guns on their legs, they would be only too glad of an excuse to use.

And he was Sheriff of the county!

He smothered an oath beneath his breath, and resolved to get busy pronto on the rustling angle. He said, "Buck, I reckon we'll just stick Tumbleweed onto that job. He's the logical candidate for it anyhow, 'cause he's already got a foothold in Borst's camp. Right now, I'm countin' heavy on him to get us news if Borst tries to pull anythin' slick. He—"

"This here Tumbleweed gent," Tranter observed sourly, "ain't my idea of a up-an'-comin' law officer. He lookes more tuh me like Billy the Kid's second cousin, or mebbe Butch Cassidy's twin brother."

"Do I know the gentleman?" Jones asked, interested.

"Nope," Tranter growled, "but he's a brand fer the burnin', an' it mightn't do no harm if yuh looked 'im up."

"If you *do* see him," Bill cautioned, "don't let anythin' drop about him bein' one of my deputies. There ain't nothin' wrong with him," he added, "except his feet ain't twins an' Nature sold him short when it come to passelin' out the looks. But I reckon he's honest."

"Yeah—yuh oughta be a parson yoreself," Tranter jeered, "yuh're that optimistic!"

"It is man's duty to give his fellows the benefit of any doubt," Jones reminded gently.

"Tuh my way o' thinkin'," said Tranter sourly, getting to his feet, "yuh c'd give that pilgrim the benefit o' *all* the doubts an' he *still* would stink! But you'll learn—by the time they're shov'lin dirt in yore face. Wisht I c'd recollect where I seen that skinny wart before . . ." He jingled thoughtfully toward the swinging doors. "Well, anyhow, yuh mark my words, Bill—that jasper an' Pecos Borst is thicker'n splatter. He'll be hookin' the linin' plumb off'n yore silver cloud, less'n yuh cut loose of him pronto."

XIII / *BORST STRIKES BACK*

Dorne grinned at Gospel Jones as Tranter passed through the Broken Harp's batwing doors. "Buck," he chuckled, "is about as happy as a bloodhound's eye. Never see such a fella for throwin' cold water an' hangin' crepe. His food mustn't sit real well. Always preachin' calamity—"

"An' he can dish it out, too," Jones cut in grimly. "You don't want to underrate Tranter, Bill. He's daunsy, all right," he admitted, rasping a calloused hand across his beard-stubbled chin reminiscently, "but he's seen a lot of the seamy side of life. He's done most of his travellin' as you might say, among the Philistines—an' Buck's a man who believes the old sayin' about Rome. He's been around, Bill. His name's been carved on more'n one Boothill epitaph."

Dorne looked at the rangeland parson curiously. "Yeah?"

"Uh-huh. Such epitaphs as this—'Ed Lock was buried here. Ed was rated pronto quick till Brimstone Tranter slowed him down.' I can remember Ed pretty well. Reckon I ought to; he was a holy terror to Bible-packers down in Texas. Yes, Bill, Tranter's been around. I've heard of him over in New Mexico, too, one place an' another. He's left his mark on this Western country. I've heard he come from Missouri when he wasn't knee-high to a jackrabbit. But he got his early rearin' down Tombstone way. His father was a frontier marshal. A close friend, they say, of Doc Holliday an' Wyatt Earp. Buck always had a wild streak in him, though. Restless, he was, an' always wantin' to be up an' doin'. When things was quiet he'd sort of drift away to turn up five-six months later, clear across the state—or outside of it. Between you an' me, I don't reckon he's always kep' his feet on the straight an' narrow."

Dorne nodded thoughtfully. "It don't make no never-mind to me, though," he offered. "What a man's been is his own business, the way I look at it. I usu'lly judge a man by what he is an' what he does when I know him."

Gospel Jones said, "You're right, too. What a man has been in the past is between him and his God. It's the present that counts the most. No man is perfect. The Lord don't expect it. Let a man repent, make restitution in so far as he is able, and—"

Jones broke off as a short, squatty puncher with squinty eyes and bulbous nose pushed through the crowd and paused before their table. "One of you gents the Sheriff?" he muttered.

"I am," Dorne answered, looking the man over closely. You lookin' for me?"

"I'm not, but there's a fella over in yore office what is. Fella named Krayson. Used tuh work for the Wineglass—"

Bill shoved back from the table and got to his feet. "See you later," he said to Jones, and hurried toward the entrance. Shoving through the batwings, he reached the porch and paused, dropping to its warped planking as a burst of lurid flame beat outward from the horse-packed hitch rail fronting the resort.

When Dorne's body struck the porch flooring he rolled for the steps and down them, getting out his pistol as he did so. When he came to a stop on the plank walk he surged to his feet, the gun weaving in his hand as startled pedestrians scuttled for shelter. Bill had not been hit, but a slug had pierced the crown of his Stetson and another had ripped through the fluttering ends of his lavender neckerchief. And he was mad—plenty mad!

But the fellow had got clear away before he'd come to his feet. He could have heard the fellow's pounding boots, he felt, had not so many other gents been running at the time, in an effort to get out of any possible line of fire. As it was, the would-be assassin had made good his escape.

With a smothered oath, Bill strode back inside, shoving men off his elbows as they crowded round the door with expectant eyes. "Nobody hurt," he growled. "Don't block this entrance—there might be *another* fire."

Ortega was standing at Venta's side not five feet from the door and in direct line with a window overlooking the porch. Venta's swarthy features paled, as he found Bill's glance upon him and the meaning in Bill's words grew clear. Bill's cold grin fired up his face and made it reckless. "You better have more luck next time, 'cause it'll be the last chance you'll get," he drawled, and left Venta and his friend to digest this at their leisure.

He strode straight to the Sheriff's Office and found the place dark. He approached it cautiously. No telling what might happen next. It struck him suddenly that the whole thing was bait to get him into the light from the flaring torches affixed to the front of the Broken Harp, where that dry-gulching killer could have a chance to earn his money. It was dollars to doughnuts, he told himself bitterly, that Krayson hadn't been within a block of this office.

He'd swallowed the line, sinker and all. Only Providence, or the bushwhacker's hurried aim, had saved him. He'd acted like a damnfool kid. Small wonder folks called him wild!

He paused at one side of the open office door and listened for a full five minutes before, satisfied that the place was empty, he entered with a snort of disgust. Moving toward the wall beside his desk, he reached up and found the lamp bracketed to the wall. He removed its chimney and struck a match. When the wick flared up he replaced the chimney and—

Wham!

The echoes of the shot drowned the tinkle of

shattered glass. In total darkness Dorne crouched where he had whirled, facing the open door. Then, at the sound of running feet, he made for the door with angry strides. Twice was too many times to be made a target of in the same half-hour! Somebody was going to be shown it did not pay to monkey with the Sheriff of Spavined Nag!

He reached the doorway and was through it in three swift steps. Too bad there wasn't more light on this side of the street. Some drunken fool must have shot up the lantern that was customarily lit above the doorway of the express office two doors to the right. He paused abruptly to try and catch the direction of those running feet.

It was all that saved him, that pause!

There was a *thwunk!* He flicked a glance across his shoulder and in the reflected light from the honkytonks across the street he saw the vibrating gleam of steel. A knife—imbedded in the wall at his side, on a level with his chest!

He knew where that had come from! The blade had been thrown from the mouth of the alley running between the express office and the building in between. A saddle shop; closed.

Dorne wasted scant time in thought. Even as these things blurred through his mind, he was reaching down with his left hand and removing the spurs and danglers from his high-heeled boots. Then, weaving forward with cat-footed stride, he rounded the far corner of the Sheriff's Office and found things black as the inside of a dead cow's stomach. This was not so good, but he consoled himself with the thought that what he couldn't see, that ornery knife-thrower could not see, either.

Realizing the need for caution here, unless he wished the feel of a slithering blade between his ribs, Dorne advanced slowly down the alley between the office and the jail, making toward where the alley used by the knife-wielder opened upon it.

Every few steps he stopped to listen. Once he imagined he heard a pebble crunch beneath a booted foot, but he could not be sure. From afar came the muted sound of off-key music from one of the resorts, and the sing-song drone of the prompter. But in this alley it was still as death.

In the swirling gloom, Dorne's jaws were clenched and his wide lips thinned and determined. Three attempts in one night on the same man's life was carrying things too far! Before he got through, he allowed he was going to make some durn jasper realize it wasn't safe to play such pranks with Wild Bill Dorne.

Where in hell *was* that squirt? Standing motionless with bated breath, Dorne could hear no slightest sound of stealthy bootstep. Nor could he hear the subdued breathing of the unseen skulker. Had the fellow, like his predecessors, got away?

And just then, through the blanketing darkness,

an outstretched hand with a knife in it came up against Dorne's cheek softly.

Dorne's reaction was instantaneous and even swifter than was that of the hand's owner. Up came Bill's gun-weighted right in a smashing arc that crunched suddenly against flesh and bone—but it was only the assassin's shoulder. And the left shoulder, at that. As Dorne realized a second later when the knife's dull glint bit a sweeping circle a scant inch short of his chin.

Shouts and the pound of running feet in front of the Sheriff's Office told Dorne now that men had been attracted by the shot that had smashed the lamp. But he gave them no portion of his attention. He was engaged in an encounter with an unknown adversary whom he felt sure would like nothing better than to plant his naked steel in some vital part of the Sheriff's anatomy.

This intuition fanned the flame of Dorne's fierce temper and made him suddenly reckless. Throwing back his right clenched fist, he reached forward in a circular motion with his left. But it did not touch the unseen knifeman. *Where had the fellow gone?*

Bill knew the next moment when the fellow's steel ripped his sleeve from wrist to elbow! With a smothered oath, Bill let drive with his right, gun-weighted fist. It struck the would-be assassin a punishing blow, drove him staggering back. Bill could hear his laboured panting as he sought to keep his feet. But even as the man went lurching backward, he must have flung his blade. For Dorne heard its whistle and felt its breath as it passed between his extended arm and his right side. He heard it *chunk!* against the building two feet away, and vibrate wickedly.

Sure that he had the fellow now, Bill went plunging forward. And his chin plowed through the dust as he tripped over the marauder's lowcrouched form. And the breath was for a moment knocked completely out of him. It was his antagonist's chance, and the fellow took it. Though not as Bill had expected—his bootheels thumped out a swift retreat.

As Bill picked himself out of the dust a moment later, he realized why. The light of an up-held lantern came round the opposite corner of the building, and behind it came a shadowy group of men with determined faces. There were two or three swiftly indrawn breaths and a couple of muted oaths as these citizens caught sight of Dorne.

"Suff'rin' sidewinders!" Tranter snapped, and lowered his lantern. "We thought they'd got yuh that time! What the heck's been happenin' round here?"

Bill told them tersely. The men, solid citizens, shook their heads. "We heered that shot," Tranter told him. "Heered about that trouble yuh had in front of the Broken Harp, too. I didn't figure

Borst would crawl off with his tail 'tween his laigs—an' he ain't. This is some of his doin's; yuh kin bank on it! Them hellions won't rest till yo're planted—"

"An' I ain't figurin' to rest," Dorne said, "till I've run them rannyhans clear outa the country! So you can look forward to a right uproarious time!"

XIV / WET-BLANKETED CATTLE

Back inside the office, and with the shades drawn down to the sills and the front door closed as an added precaution, Buck Tranter said to Dorne:

"I been talkin' a mite with the Gospel-slinger. That fella kin use his eyes; he give me a chin-picture of this hombre what told yuh Krayson was waitin' in yore office that was dang near good as them what these jaspers with a black box an' a tripod takes. That mealy-mouthed liar was that sawed-off squirt of a Dode Harniss—the guy which owned the knife Fisk was packin' in his pocket."

"I'd begun," Bill said, "to figure as much myself."

Tranter nodded, and getting out his battered pipe, said: "It was. You got any spare tobacco, Bill? I'm fresh out an' this yere hod needs exercise."

Dorne eyed the pipe distastefully, but passed over his sack of Durham. "You got any idea what Harniss passed me that word for?"

Tranter, packing his pipe, grinned. "It's as clear as the nose on yore map, Bill. He was figurin' to git yuh outside where Krayson, hidin' 'mongst them hawsses by the hitch rack, could snuff yore light with a minymum of danger."

"Sure—but *why?*"

"Don't ast me questions like that. I ain't good at riddles. Lemme ast you one. If a hawss is sixteen hands high, got a mean eye an' a long Roman nose, an' weighs round 'leven hundred pounds, how old's his rider?"

Bill snorted. "I'll ask the questions," he growled. "I can answer 'em, too," he added grimly. "Harniss an' Krayson joined them rustlers of their own accord—if they wasn't already hooked up with 'em! Otherwise, they wouldn't be walkin' round this place leadin' solid citizens into trouble; they'd be dead or prisoners."

"Sounds reasonable," Tranter admitted, puffing out a thick blue cloud of aromatic smoke through which he eyed Bill sharply. "I kin add tuh that. Harniss has been a two-bit rustler ever since I've knowed him."

"Why didn't you tell me that right off?" Bill growled.

"A wise man," Tranter grinned, "keeps his lip buttoned an' don't do no oratin' outa turn. I recollect a fella once what talked himself into a decoration fer a cottonwood branch."

Bill snorted. "You go over to the printer's—he sleeps out back of his place—an' get him to run you off two-three hundred flyers offerin' a hundred-an'-fifty bucks reward for information leadin' to the arrest an' conviction of Dode Harniss an' Ed Krayson, ex–Wineglass punchers, wanted for participatin' in the wholesale rustlin' of Wineglass cattle. When he runs 'em off, I want to see that they get tacked up in prominent places—*quick*. Get at it."

"Jest a second," Tranter grunted, getting to his feet and knocking out his pipe. "You got any idee who that knifeman was?"

"I got a sneakin' notion," Bill said, "that it was Pedro Mendota. I'm figurin' to look him up right now. "An'," he added ominously, "if he can't give a damn good account of his movements for the last coupla hours, somethin' unpleasant is goin' to happen."

Bill went over Spavined Nag with the proverbial fine-toothed comb, but he did not find the wily Mendota, nor anyone who would admit they'd seen him all evening. It was mighty irritating. If he could only have laid hands on the fellow, Bill believed he would have got a considerable distance toward the solution of his troubles. If Mendota himself had not been mixed up with the rustling operations being carried on in the vicinity, Bill believed the Mexican could have given him the names of a number of gents who were. But now that the swarthy gun fighter had vanished, he could not put this notion to the test.

He did, however, visit the Broken Harp and Ortega's Black Bottle Bar—the town's two largest resorts, now that he had put the Golden Stack into the limbo of forgotten joints. In these two dives

Bill read the riot act. If, he drawled, another shooting, knifing, or other form of fracas took place in either, he would serve them the same potent dose he'd given Borst's Golden Stack! And it was plain that he meant exactly what he said.

Three days slid by, and then, early on the morning of the fourth, a white-faced rider swept into town on a winded, lathered bronc. Hitting dirt on skidding boot-heels, this panting buckaroo banged his boots across the boardwalk, pelted up the steps and came jingling into the Sheriff's Office, where he jarred to a sudden stop. There was a wild look in his eyes, and breath was coming in panted gasps that shook his wiry body.

"Take it easy," Bill advised. "I'll still be here when you get yore wind."

"Heck, yes," Tranter added. "Rome wa'n't built in no day, an' it's too dang hot in this country tuh rush yuh're life away. Jest take it easy, pilgrim—we'll bear with yuh."

"Listen!" the puncher gasped. "Listen—Borst's raised hell right, an' shoved a chunk under it! He's gone mad as a hatter!"

Dorne looked from the rider's trail-grimed counteance to Tranter. And back again. Then he got up and took a pace or two about the room, his hands deep-thrust in the leather pockets of his chaps.

He said, "S'pose you chew it finer, pardner. An'

remember that jestin' lies usually bring serious sorrows."

"Ain't it the truth?" Tranter butted in. "I recollect the time—"

"Recollect this ain't the time to tell it then," Dorne growled, and looked at the rider again. "Well?"

"It's like I said. Borst's gone clean off his button. Some folks has allus suspicioned that he's had a hand in this wholesale rustlin' that's been goin' on, but nobody ever hoped tuh prove it. Ain't no need of provin' it, now! His spread's plumb lousy with rustled steers! I was comin' through there—through his south-west range—late yestiday afternoon, an' I shore seen plenty! Blotched brands all over the hills!"

"What brand of likker do yuh drink?" Tranter cut in, when the buckaroo paused for breath.

"Ol' Crow—why?"

"By cripes, I'm gonna order me a barrel. Bill, that's the kinda stuff we oughta equip this yere office with. Must be marv'lous!"

"Say!" the rider snarled, "yuh don't think I'm lyin', do yuh?"

Bill said, "Well, I don't know you well enough for that. But it wouldn't surprise me none if this was yore idea of humour."

"Humour!" the fellow snorted, and ripped out a couple of choice oaths. "Humour—hell! I'm tellin' you there's rustled critters on the Hashknife

range. I seen 'em with my own eyes. An' by cripes I guess I know what I'm seein' when I see it!"

"Shucks," Tranter drawled. "Fer all we know, yuh couldn't tell a hawk from a handsaw. What spread you ridin' for?"

"Them that sows brambles better not be goin' round barefoot!" the fellow growled, a resentful glint in his eye. "You dang stringbean! Fer two cents I'd work you over! What spread am I ridin' for? I *own* my brand; the Bar B 4—my steers is thicker'n cloves on a Christmas ham! Where in hell did you come from?"

Bill said quickly, before Tranter had a chance to answer:

"Where do *you* come from?"

"Sunset County—an' thank Gawd the lawmen over there ain't dumb as you two yaps!"

"Yaps, is it?" Tranter started rolling up his sleeves.

But Bill pushed him back in his chair. Bill said, "Sunset County, eh? Well, would you mind oratin' how-come yo're tellin' me about yore troubles? If yore star-packers is so all-fired up-an'-comin', seems like you'd do well to pack this grief to them."

The owner of the Bar B 4 threw his hat down and jumped on it. "By George, I didn't know *any* county—even Spavined Nag—paid good hard cash for such poor excuses of peace officers as you birds!" He divided a scathing glance between them, adding, *"Borst's ranch is in yore county, ain't it?"*

Bill swallowed his resentment at the other's abuse abruptly. Borst's spread *was* in Spavined Nag territory, at that—unfortunately. Before he could answer, however, Tranter said from his position by the window:

"Another jasper bulgin' down the road! Cripes, this place is gettin' busier than a flea with pups!"

Bill whirled to the window, took one look and said, "Ol' Man Globe!"

"The Mayor?" the stranger growled.

"Yeah."

"Mebbe I'll git some action, then—unless he's petrified, too!"

"Brother, I'd admire tuh know yore handle," Tranter purred softly. "Some day when I ain't so busy—and the climate's cooled off a bit—I'm allowin' tuh look you up."

"Bar B Smith, that's me. An' yuh can look any damned time yuh want to," the man who drank Old Crow snapped belligerently. "Any time you're a-figerin' tuh pack a quarrel my way, jest fork yore bronc an' come a-foggin'."

Globe slid from his skidding horse outside the door and came clumping in on the double-quick. "Bill," he panted, "Borst's come into the open. I seen sixteen head of rustled critters on his no'theast range!"

Dorne swore. "What is this, anyway? I'm as

anxious to smash Pecos Borst as you gents are to have me, but—"

Tranter said in reply to Globe's surprised look, "That bow-legged jigger claims *he* saw smears of rustled steers on Hashknife's south-west range." And, strangely, he grinned a bit as he said it, as though pleased at some secret joke.

"That clinches it," Globe muttered. "Borst's come into the open. Must think he's so big we don't dare tackle him—but he'll find out diff'rent. Get a posse, Bill! We'll go right—"

"Hold on a second," Bill said flatly. "I'm still sheriffin' this county. Let me get this straight, now. How many rustled steers did you see?" he looked at Globe. "An' just where? An' how you know they're rustled?"

The Mayor gulped, and glared. "Listen," he spluttered, "when I say I seen rustled cattle, you can bet yore damn boots I seen 'em!"

"All right," Bill said. "Where?"

"Near the mouth of Hards' Pass Draw! Sixteen of 'em—hand-counted an' hand-runnin'!"

Bill nodded. "How'd you know they was rustled?"

"How do I know I got my own hat on!" Mayor Globe snorted. "A fine son-in-law you'll make! Don't you s'pose I know my own steers? S'pose I can't tell a blotched brand when I see one? *Hell!*"

"Yeah," snarled Bar B Smith. "That's what *I* say!" He glared at Bill vindictively, and snapped at Globe, "How'd yuh ever come tuh make a sheriff outa such poor material?"

Bill grunted to Tranter, "C'mon—let's go!" and started for the door.

Tranter followed, a saturnine twinkle in his faded eyes. Behind him stamped Bar B Smith and the Mayor of Spavined Nag.

Bill wasn't as slow on the pick-up as he had let on—not by a darned sight. But, unable to believe his ears at such good luck as a slip like this on the part of the slick and crooked Borst, he had wanted to make absolutely sure.

If he went out there half-cocked, Borst would make him the laughing-stock of the whole blamed country.

But, now that it seemed Borst actually had made such a bull, he intended letting no grass grow under his boots. Although he was still a mite sceptical. Globe and Smith, he felt, might actually have seen what they claimed they saw. But the chances of those rustled cattle being on the premises when they got there, was something else again!

Nevertheless, hardly ten minutes later, he, Tranter, Globe, Smith and three other fight-loving possemen headed out of town on fresh broncs along the trail that led to Pecos Borst's Hashknife outfit, some thirty miles away.

In the book and print-lined office of his ranch house on the Hashknife range, Pecos Borst strode nervously up and down the room, an unlighted cigar gripped savagely in one corner of his thick-lipped mouth, a smoky light in the depths of his frowning eyes.

Pecos Borst was feeling ringey as a sore-pawed wolf.

And with good cause, he thought malignantly. Every stride was packed with venom and an ominous threat might be read in the forward throw of his massive shoulders. Indeed, it was read there by the silent watcher across the room.

Phoenix John Muroc, Borst's chief gambler, sat over there in a cowhide chair, the consumptive pallor of his bony features emphasized by the glow from the yellow lamp. For over an hour Muroc had been sitting there, content to hold his silence while he watched the big man pacing back and forth.

Nor did he speak now until Borst growled:

"How long you figger Mendota's been gone, Phoenix?"

" 'Bout two hours, I'd allow."

"Then he's had time to learn the straight of it. Oughta be back here any minute. An' he better," he added ominously. "I tell you, I don't get this! Pete swears he ain't put no critters on that part of the range. If Pete ain't lyin', who the hell put 'em there?"

"Couldn't say," Muroc answered. "But I don't reckon Mendota's stretchin' things when he claims he ain't drove no steers onto the north-east nor south-west fodder. He'd know better'n to pull a cropper like that. You can bet he tucked them steers away in some hidden box canyon or gulch back in the hills."

"Then what in blazes are they doin' on my range where some damn fool can see 'em an' hotfoot the information to that damn Dorne?"

Phoenix John saw no use in answering that. *He didn't know.*

For some minutes longer Borst continued his savage pacing of the floor, so many steps this way, so many steps that. At last he paused to wheel toward the lamp on the table in the corner, pulling a crumpled envelope from his coat pocket as he did so. From this he pulled a soiled bit of cheap notepaper on which several lines had been scrawled with a blunt pencil. For the twentieth time he read them:

"*Deer Pecos:*

If you got any regard fer yore skin, you'll move them blotched critters what's feedin' in large numbers on yore north-east an south-west range.

A FRIEND."

For the twentieth time Borst's beefy face flamed with rage. "By Gawd, if there is rustled cattle on my spread, I'm gonna make mince-meat outa the guy what put 'em there! I'm gonna—"

Out of the side of his bitter mouth Muroc said, "Rider comin'."

"What—?" Borst thrust the letter into his pocket and wheeled to watch the door, one hand at his side within fast reaching distance of the heavy Colt that swung in the holster against his hip. "Must be Pete."

It was. The door swung open abruptly and Pedro Mendota stepped swiftly into the room, the glint of anger in his snapping glance. "Señor Borst, it ees the trut' what that note say! The range, she ees covaired weeth them cattle we wet-blanketed!"

XV / *BORST RECEIVES A VISIT*

For a long second there was silence, a thick and dangerous stillness through which Borst eyed his Mexican lieutenant with a glance that would have curled up many another hardy soul like a dead leaf. But not the dust-stained Mendota, whose swarthy face abruptly creased in a laugh that was smooth and easy, the while he shrugged his graceful shoulders. "But the luck, Señor, she ees due for change. No man can have soch bad luck forevair."

Borst scowled the attempted consolation aside with an oath that crackled.

He snarled, "Did you have sense enough to get hold of your men an' start 'em hazing that rustled stock off somewheres where it wouldn't be seen?"

"But yes, Señor—*seguro si.*" Mendota put his panther-lean hips against the wall and crossed his chap-clad legs. He rolled a cigarette with a swift left-handed nonchalance. Snapped a match to flame with his right thumbnail and held an end of his brown-paper smoke above it; when it caught and was going, he put its other end in his mouth. He watched Borst through its upward-drifting smoke.

When it became apparent that Borst was waiting for further and more detailed information, Pedro Mendota supplied it with an easy assurance. "I have left Gleed, Krayson, Harniss an' that Tumbleweed to drive them dogies off."

"That Tumbleweed," the pale-faced Phoenix John cut in, "is an odd stick—uncommon odd. Talks too damn much without sayin' nothin'. Who the hell is he? Where'd he come from? How do you know he ain't a spy from the Cattlemen's Association? Or a pussy-footin' keyholer from the Sheriff's Office?"

Borst smiled thinly. "You don't need to worry about him." He turned his big shoulders back toward the Mexican, and his smoky eyes regarded him unblinkingly from beneath his sleepy lids. "Then you think we needn't worry none about this business, eh?"

Mendota grinned "Why should we? We have nevair worried before."

The flame of some inner heat lay a line of colour across Borst's heavy jowls. "If I ever locate the skunk that hazed them critters into the open," he said, "I'll cut strips from his gizzard an' ram 'em down his throat!"

Mendota shrugged, and his teeth showed whitely against the swarthy copper of his face. "*Por Dios*, I shall help you," he smiled, and his dark little eyes were alive with flashing sparkles.

"If he'd nine lives," growled Phoenix John, "I'd snuff each one with a slow pleasure an' then feel sorry he hadn't more! D'you suppose it's Wild Bill Dorne?"

Borst shook his head contemptuously, as though such an idea was unworthy of sober thought. "How could that profit him? He—"

Phoenix John broke in:

"It would give him a swell chance to railroad you!"

Borst's expression showed that he was giving the idea attention. Then, "Where's Lola?" he demanded suddenly.

Mendota shrugged. Muroc said, "I ain't got no idea."

Borst stuck his head out the door, shouted something into the thickening dusk. A man came running up from the bunkhouse. Borst said: "Hunt up Lola, an' when you find 'er, send 'er in here." The fellow departed, and Borst withdrew his head and shut the door. "I don't like the way that skirt's been actin' lately. I got half a notion she's fallin' for that damned Bill Dorne. A fella oughtn't use women in this game; they're a heap too blamed uncertain. You was suggestin', John . . . ?"

"I was sayin' that if Dorne happened to think of it, an' knew where we was holdin' them cattle, he mighta been the one to shove 'em onto our open range. It would give him a chance to 'discover' 'em. *That* would give him what he's been lookin' for all long—the chance to railroad you to the pen!"

"It would, yeah," Borst answered slowly. "If he could cut it. But I don't think Dorne did it; it ain't his style. He's the kinda fool who plays straight out from the shoulder. No," he shook his head, "I don't reckon Bill done it. An' if nobody's seen 'em an' forked a bronc into town to spread the news, it's a heap likely he don't know about 'em yet."

"Well, I wouldn't count on it, was I you," Muroc growled sourly.

Before Borst could reply, had he been of a mind to, the jingling clump of spurred and booted feet announced the approach of someone. Came a knock on the door and, at Borst's soft "Come in," one of the Hashknife punchers—a burly ruffian—came into the room. Before he spoke he shot a cold glance about the room, which seemed to rest longest and with an open disapproval upon the Mexican gun fighter, Mendota.

Then, as his glance swung round to Borst, he said, "That skirt ain't on the place."

The quickening of Borst's high blood laid a pronounced flush across his cheeks. His long, smoke-coloured eyes grew cloudy, muddy as the darkening thoughts churned round in that wide, high, florid forehead. His big, rocklike figure seemed to tense, to expand. Then, unexpectedly, he chuckled deep down in his bull throat. And it was not a pleasant sound.

"So!" he purred. "So that's her game, is it. By Gawd, I'll bloody well wring that ivory neck of hers if she don't kick clean." And his lips made a sinister curve against the tautness of his face.

Without quite knowing why, the puncher shivered. Borst's gaze was on him squarely. Borst said, "Are you sure?"

"You can have some other hairpin take a look if you don't think so," the puncher blustered, to cover the embarrassment he felt at his momentary exhibition of weakness by shivering under Borst's regard.

The boss of Spavined Nag said, "I ain't in the habit of havin' a second gent check the work I set another bird to do."

"That's all right with me," the puncher growled. "I looked an' she ain't here. Anyways I'm gettin' plumb fed up with workin' fer promises. That," and he swung a truculent stare toward Mendota, "blasted breed ain't paid—"

But he got no further, for at that precise moment Mendota's right hand dropped to the brass-studded holster that sagged his gunbelt at the centre. There was a spit of flame, a loud report and the puncher abruptly doubled up and pitched face downward across the floor.

Mendota said nothing, but his eyes were on Borst closely as, with an appearance of nonchalance, he blew the smoke from his gun and replaced the spent cartridge with a fresh one from his belt. Whether by accident or design he seemed to forget to put the gun away, and its muzzle remained slightly tilted in the direction of Pecos Borst.

Phoenix John Muroc licked dry lips with an edge of his pink tongue. But Borst's grin licked a thin line across his mouth and he said "Fast work," with a peculiar husky softness to his tones. And—

"You were right, Pete; we can't have insubordination in the ranks."

"No sabe that word, *señor*," Mendota smiled. "But if you mean we cannot pay the fools who work for us, *por Dios*, that ees all right weeth me. But don' forget, *señor*, there ees a pleasure which ees born of pain. Do not try to double-cross weeth Pedro Mendota—he expects for to get the pay." And that grin on his lips curled wickedly as he stared at Pecos Borst.

Borst shrugged. "You'll get paid," he said easily. "Stick with me a spell longer, Pete, an' we'll show a few wise guys a couple of things. I ain't done in this country by one hell of a long ways." His smoky eyes played over the Mexican's panther-lithe figure. He said with a casualness that did not deceive anyone:

"By the way, Pete; how come you shot that sage-brusher at the Black Bottle the other day?"

"Gov'ment agent," Mendota said laconically.

Borst's eyes showed interest. "A Federal man? How'd you get onto him?"

"He was sneak around two-three times where I been. I watch heem. See heem talk with many hombres in the low voice. I put two an' two togethair. She spell gov'ment man to me."

Borst nodded thoughtfully, his glance on the raftered ceiling as though in speculation. Outside the night was thickening, cooling off, taking on mystery and enchantment in the light of the rising moon.

From afar came the faint, dim flutter of many hoofs; sometimes they swelled a little in volume, as though their owners had carried them up out of some distant valley. Then they would dim again. But always, as they swelled, their volume perceptibly heightened as though the unseen mounts were nearing.

The three men exchanged silent glances, and unuttered thoughts shone from the eyes of each.

Borst said abruptly, "If that's Dorne, you birds take yore cues from me. This ain't no time for slip-ups. Don't either of you crack a smile unless I give the sign."

With a springy step he moved to the window overlooking the yard. "Douse that light," he growled.

It was in darkness then—darkness save for what pale light the moon shed down—that Borst and his two companions watched the arrival of a group of shadowy horsemen who slid their broncs to a halt just short of the veranda steps, and hit dirt with the creak of released saddle leather and clink of jingling spurs.

From out of this blurred huddle rose a voice. "D'yuh reckon anybody's home?"

And another voice called, "Hallo the house! You home, Borst?"

"It's him," Borst growled, and swore.

XVI / "YALLER AS A MONGREL PUP!"

"Fetch a lamp," Borst said, and said it softly. When Muroc brought him one, Mendota not stirring so much as a finger, Borst snapped a match to flame and lit it. "Stay in here till I give the word an' have yore guns where you can get at 'em handy." With the lamp in hand he started for the door, reached and opened it, and strode blinking out upon the veranda.

"Howdy, gents," he said then, easily. "What's all the excitement? Dorne eloped with that yellow-haired Lola-girl?"

Came a muttered imprecation, and then Dorne's own voice:

"Not this time, Pecos. I'm here on business. An' it's connected with you. Comes plumb close to you, it does, an' I'm allowin' you better be right careful what yuh do an' what yuh say."

"You sure can paint 'er creepy."

"It's a creepy subject," Dorne said flatly. "Borst, the sand in yore clock of time's about run out. How many more minutes you got left is likely to be determined by yore ability to talk." He paused to let this sink in and then, as Borst said nothing, added: "First thing I crave to know is how'd yore brand get on so many rustled cattle?"

By the light of the lamp in his hand, Borst's

features registered surprise. "What rustled cattle you talkin' about, Bill?"

Dorne gave him a hard glance, and Dorne's glance was emulated by a number of others directed at Borst. Borst saw them all and felt a vague uneasiness that was not as vague as he could and would have wished. "Has somebody been stealin' cattle?"

"You know damn well," Dorne snapped, "somebody has. An' if I ain't gone plumb stark an' ravin' crazy, you know durned well who the somebody is!"

"Where are these critters?"

"On yore south-west an' north-east ranges—or at least they was. Right now, I reckon they're sorta driftin' looselike clean across this patch o' prairie. Back where they come from, I shouldn't wonder. I come across some of yore friends actually tryin' to tool 'em outa sight. But they was a little slow, an' the cattle was tired. I seen 'em, all right, so there ain't no use you trying to lie out of it; they was somebody else's steers, an' they had yore brand slapped over their rightful marks. Do you plead guilty or—"

"You been elected judge an' jury for this county as well as Sheriff?" Borst asked with a sour dryness.

"Where I come from," cut in a voice Borst recognized as belonging to the ragged deputy, Tranter, "we don't waste no time with cattle thiefs. We string 'em up to the nearest branch!"

"Slow down, Buck," Dorne said. "This kinda business has to be done all smooth an' legal-like. The law says cattle rustlers shall be given fair trial, same as any other kind of snake. Borst, you got anythin' to say for yoreself?"

"Sure I have," Borst came back, shoving his jaw out belligerently. "I got a lot to say, Mister. Such raw stuff as this can't be pulled an' got away with. You know well as I do that I never stole them steers—if any's *been* stole!" he added nastily. "I been right here in the house ever since you ordered me away from town, an' before that you know damn well I never had no chance to go gallopin' round the range slappin' my mark on other folks' cattle."

"Sure, I know you didn't do it personal, Pecos. But if you hadn't been standin' back of the ornery bunch of whippoorwills what done it, they wouldn't of had the nerve. You're guilty as they are, Borst—guilty as hell."

"An'," Tranter threw in, "yuh're goin' ter make what the story-books calls the 'supreem sacryfice'!"

"Right!" snapped Mayor Globe. "Unloosen his collar, Buck."

"I wouldn't advise any of you gents to make a false move—any kind of a move, in fact. There's two of my men in the house with guns trained right on you birds. That's what I got this light for—to make good targets out of you. Hell, if you'd had a gram of sense," Borst sneered, "you'd have known you couldn't run no blazer like this on Pecos Borst!"

"Listen at the coyote," Tranter jeered. "Do yuh think we're scared of yore damn gunmen? Let 'em shoot! Tuh hell with 'em!" And with the words Tranter started forward, hand extended for Borst's collar.

But it didn't get there—not just then. One of the punchers beside Tranter was moving forward, too. And he was between Tranter and the house. From a flanking window a gun went off abruptly, smashing its echoes across the night stillness, blasting the puncher beside the ragged deputy off his feet and down on his face in a gurgling sob.

Tranter swore and his right hand went streaking down as both Borst's hands went up above his head in a sign of peace. Flame licked out from Tranter's hip, chunked viciously into something inside and beyond the window. But it wasn't a man his lead had targeted, for all could hear the hurried pound of booted feet that heralded swift evacuation by Borst's allies.

Snapping out his orders into the milling huddle of his posse, Dorne sprang up the steps and through the door, two possemen at his heels. Borst felt something hard dig into the folds of his paunchy stomach and, looking down, saw that it was Tranter's gun. Saw, too, the wicked smirk on Tranter's lips. "One hurried breath," Tranter said, "an' yore light goes out—an' I ain't referrin' to the light in that there lamp!"

"You ain't heard the last of this," Borst purred. "I wouldn't be surprised to learn that you're mixed up in these rustled cattle somehow—"

"You ain't far from right, at that," Tranter said, and chuckled. "But I ain't the gent what slapped them crooked brands on. An' I don't need tuh hire no Kraysons nor Harnisses tuh do my dirty work—nor no damn back-shootin', bushwhackin' Pedro Mendotas. That's one of the diff'rences between you an' me."

Borst turned his attention to the possemen searching the surrounding brush, to the possemen herding the Hashknife crew from the bunkhouse—such of the crew as occupied it, anyway. And Borst's lips curled as he watched and listened. And that which he listened for he wasn't long in hearing—the swift rataplan of hard-hammering hoofs as Mendota and Phoenix John lay low along their horses' necks in a dash to elude the shouting, swearing possemen who now came running for their broncs.

With a sudden twist of his heavy body Borst shook free of the pistol in Tranter's hand, threw himself backward and sent his lamp hurtling straight into the huddled group of snorting posse horses. The startled broncs yanked their reins from the grip of the men delegated to hold them and went scattering away in half a dozen different directions. That was the last thing Borst saw for a number of minutes, for just then Tranter brought the barrel of his gun down squarely on Borst's wide forehead and everything went black. Yet, even as he fell, Borst laughed.

Borst came back to reality with the knowledge that rough hands were jerking him to his feet, and that a rougher hand was slapping him across the face in a way that stung. He opened his eyes with a mounting rage and found Bill Dorne's face squarely in his vision. And Bill Dorne's face reflected an anger at least as great as his own. Recollection came then, and Borst laughed.

Dorne's blue eyes went cold and bleak. "That trick, Mister, is goin' to cost you something."

"Yeah?"

"You'll know it!" By light of the lantern held in Tranter's hand Borst could see that the sweat of some recent exertion had dried across Bill Dorne's rugged cheeks, gluing to them the powdery grit of alkali. And alkali grit was likewise plain along the edge of Dorne's red hair, where it showed beneath his shoved-back hat. Dorne's mouth was a straight white line.

"I don't have to be told who fired that shot, Pecos," Dorne said. "It was Mendota or the gent with him. I saw Mendota plain as he forked his nag. The other bird kep' his mug outa sight, but I'm bettin' strong it's Phoenix John. I'm tellin' you right now I'm gettin' out rewards for them two pronto; chargin' 'em with murder. An' as for you—"

"You ain't got a thing on me," Borst jeered.

"I got enough on you," Dorne came back, "to send you away to a place where you'll have plenty of time to think over the evil of yore ways."

"Wind!" scoffed Borst. "Bluster an' hot air, Bill. You ain't scarin' me worth a damn." And turning his shoulders toward where Tranter stood with the lantern, Borst added, "As for you, fella, you better hunt yoreself a hole an' pull it in after you. 'Cause any gent that swipes Pecos Borst over the head with a pistol is goin' to be made mighty hard to find."

Tranter grinned. "What was that yuh said about hot air?"

Borst was standing on the veranda and he placed his back now against one of its roof's supporting columns. He had discerned several moments before that his holster was empty, so there was scant use in leaving his arms hang down or placing them akimbo—such a pose without a gun to back it up might be apt to seem ludicrous. Borst crossed his arms upon his chest and, though his heavy lids hid the expression of his eyes, they did nothing to lessen the steel-cold attention with which he eyed Bill Dorne and his ragged deputy. Apparently the rest of the posse had taken after Mendota and Muroc as soon as they'd recovered their ponies. To test this theory, Borst observed:

"I suppose Mendota and Phoenix John made a clean getaway."

"You better quit supposin'," Dorne growled back; "it's gonna be bad for yore health—less'n you loosen up an' admit you been engineerin' this rustling."

Borst stood with his face turned toward the wastelands off beyond Buck Tranter. Out there all the desert seemed to run together in one pale sea of sand that was wonderfully softened by the argent glow of a horned moon. In the daytime, Borst was thinking, that land out there would be a veritable inferno of baking heat. But it offered refuge. . . .

He looked at Dorne. There was nothing, he reflected, that would please him better than the feel of his own big knuckles smashing against Bill Dorne's rugged chin. Unless it was Bill Dorne's vulturine nose crunching beneath those same knuckles. The desire ran through his mind like a white-hot iron.

But Borst fought it off. Though his eagerness to avenge himself on Dorne was tumultuous, he was determined to see his enterprises, his plans and hopes in, for and about this country crowned with success. Only by holding his temper, he knew, could he hope to see that happen. Bill Dorne might be kind of dumb, he mused, but Bill Dorne was an antagonist to whom no advantage whatever could be afforded. Caution, strategy and craft must be his watchwords. He had always boasted that he was a good waiter; this fight with Dorne should prove it.

Nothing could ever hold Borst back; nothing ever had and nothing ever would!

"Oh, I don't know," he said easily. "Knowing yore cravin' for passing old saws, I expect you know the hairy one about there bein' many a slip . . . ? Might be applicable here. Worth a bit of thought, Bill. I ain't through in this country, yet. I'm still a big factor. How far do you think you'd get if you was to take me in, charged with rustlin' my neighbours' cattle?" And he smiled squarely into Dorne's flushing face.

"Not very far, mebbe," Dorne admitted with a scowl. "It's got so you just about own the courts, body an' soul. An' any jury a man'd be apt to pick, I reckon you'd have packed to the guards. Yeah, Pecos, I reckon you'd get off scot free. But I've got a sort of hankerin' to find out."

"You're wastin' yore time, Bill."

"I ain't convinced of that. I've swore to run you out or plant you, Pecos. An' I'm still aimin' to do one or the other. Like I suspected, this rustlin' business is a heap apt to miss fire if I try to ring you in as top screw. But, like I said, it's a matter open to argument, an' I reckon I'll give the thing a whirl."

Borst saw, as Dorne paused, the Sheriff's eyes upon him closely.

Dorne said across a tightening silence, "You've been this country's dawg with the brass collar long enough. There ain't been nothin' too ornery for you to touch, long as you could see a profit in it. Now, take this rustling business . . . I'm morally certain you're a rustler, Pecos. If not the king-pin, at least an egger-on and sharer-in-the-profits.

"Fact is, Pecos, I'm puttin' yore gun back in yore holster an' I'm callin' you a rustler to yore face. I'm callin' you a crawlin' Gila Monster—a thing what's lower than a snake's belly! *Now draw—if you got the guts!*"

Borst's fierce hate and rage flamed up like tow and sent the heated blood across his cheeks in a flood of colour. The smouldering eyes below his high wide forehead filled with scintillating sparks, and the knuckles of his clenched fists gleamed white as snow.

But he did not draw. Nor did either hand make the fraction of a motion toward the holster beneath his open coat where Dorne had just deposited his gun. He could feel the weight of it against his hip, but he felt no inclination to reach for it. He hated Dorne with all the power of his warped soul, but he could not bring himself to match his draw with this cold-eyed reckless sheriff.

The silence lay across the veranda like a visible thing. It was filled with unuttered thoughts, one or two of which were contemptuously framed in words:

"Hell," sneered Tranter, "there ain't a grain of sand in the baboon's craw!"

Dorne said, "Borst, you're yaller as a mongrel pup!"

"Even a *rat*," Tranter added, "will put up a scrap when cornered."

"But Borst," Bill threw in, "ain't even got the gumption of a gnat."

Borst paled. But his resentful rage, like his hatred, was a thing that could be kept and added to. It was a thing equipped with an escape-valve of caution—and that caution was shrieking now in Borst's ears like the cry of a locomotive. He *knew* that if his hand touched the pistol in his holster now, the act would be his last.

"I can wait," he muttered thickly. "I can wait."

"Then here's somethin' for you to be thinkin' over while you're doin' it," Dorne drawled. "This place is goin' to be confiscated by the law and auctioned off at a Sheriff's sale. This an' every stick, stone an' steer carryin' yore brand. It's goin' to be auctioned off to pay back the people you've been robbin'. Savvy?"

Borst said nothing, but his glittering eyes were wild with venom.

"If that won't make you fight," Bill said, coldly contemptuous, "then nothin' will. We're goin' to town an' put you in a nice warm cell. Git movin'."

XVII / *THE WOMAN SCORNED*

When Wild Bill Dorne climbed out of the saddle by the pole corral out back of the express office, both his bronc and the horse Tranter was forking were lathered with sweat and beginning to blow. Both stood there on widely braced legs, heads down, while Bill and Tranter stripped their gear off and hung it on the corral's top pole.

"It sure is hell," Tranter observed, wiping the sweat from his forehead, "but yuh'd ort to have been more careful, Bill."

"Careful!" Dorne snorted. "I'd like to know how any gent coulda been any more careful than I was. I admit I was taken in by that sidewinder's meek an' humble actions. But I was watchin' him every minute."

"Almost," Tranter corrected with a grin. "You wa'n't watchin' him any more'n I was when he run that sandy on us. We gotta keep this dark—"

"We sure have," Dorne grunted. "The reputation of this office is at stake, Buck. Why, we'd be the laughin' stock of the whole country if it ever got out Borst slid out right under our noses. We'll give out that I warned him outa the country an' he took the advice to heart an' left."

Tranter nodded dubiously. "Be all right if he really leaves, I reckon. But, yuh know, somehow I got the feelin' that vinegaroon ain't a-goin' to leave. Leastaways, not till he evens up the score fer all the hell you done raised. Cripes, you've knocked the props clean out from under his Number 12's—most of 'em, anyways. Nope, I wouldn't bank too high he's pulled his freight, Bill, was I you."

"I got that same damn feelin'," Bill admitted, with a sheepish grin. "Buck, that Borst pelican is a slippery customer."

"Slipp'rier'n calf slobbers," Tranter solemnly agreed. "An' plumb obstreperous. His crawfishin' wa'n't foolin' me a mite."

"Me neither," Dorne said, and they both laughed. Dorne sobered quickly. "You go over to the printer's an' get him to run you off a bunch of fliers offerin' one thousan' bucks apiece for the apprehension of Pedro Mendota an' Phoenix John Muroc for the killin' of a deputy sheriff while in performance of his duty. Get their description on them han' bills, too. An' the word DANGEROUS in capital letters. Get him to put the reward in red, so's it'll show up an' attract attention. I want them two hellions bad. When you get through, you can hit the hay. . . . Oh, wait a sec! Better have him run off a handful of bills advertisin' a Sheriff's sale of the Hashknife ranch property. Set the sale for . . . Let's see, to-day's Friday. Set the sale for Monday afternoon at 3 p.m."

Tranter nodded abstractedly. "Yore big mistake," he said, swinging back to the late prisoner's escape, "was in givin' Borst back his hawg-laig. If he hadn't had that gun, he wouldn't 'a' had the nerve to make a break. I only hope he's got sense enough tuh clear out fer good—but I ain't believin' it," he added pessimistically.

Dorne, with an irritable grunt, headed for the office and Tranter, thus left alone, turned the horses into the corral, rubbed them down, and clumped off toward the printer's shop.

Bill Dorne stepped into the Sheriff's Office and stopped short. He had noticed when they'd ridden into town that the light was on, but hadn't given the fact much thought. He gave it some thought now. Lola was sitting on his desk, dangling her silk-clad legs and showing them to such good effect that he caught a blushing glance of her dimpled knees.

"I thought you were never going to come," she greeted him. "Where have you been all night?"

Dorne glanced at the battered clock on the top of the safe. Three-thirty. "You hadn't ought to have hung around here all this time," he said irritably. "Folks'll be gettin' ideas."

"What do you care. After we're married—"

"Married?" Dorne cut in. "Who said anything about gettin' married?"

"Why, I thought, after the other night . . ." She let the sentence trail off and held his glance while through the silence the ticking of the clock seemed uncommonly loud. In the deep green pools of her eyes he seemed to read a vibrant, slumbering passion that was reaching out for him, that was spreading to enmesh him. As always, he sensed about her a strange magnetism. It stirred him, but he did not lose his head. He did not love this girl, and knew it. And he had no intention of letting her get away with a fast one like this.

"What you thought," he told her, "ain't the point. I never said I was going to marry you, Lola. You knew the other night that I was engaged to Marcia. What are you tryin' to do, anyway?"

"Well, I'm not trying to high-pressure you, if that's what you mean," she said scornfully. "I don't have to ask any man to marry me! I wouldn't ask the best of them. I wouldn't need to," she added fiercely. "But after the way you acted the other night, and the way you talked, I naturally supposed—"

"Well, you supposed wrong," Bill told her flatly. "I'm goin' to marry Marcia Globe."

She came to him swiftly, stood before him looking up into his face. "There's something about you that changes people, Bill." Her red lips made a long wistful curve against the alabaster pallor of her face. "I've reformed; no more cards for me. No more dance halls and honkytonks. I've quit Borst flat. An' all because of you.

"Oh, I know you never asked me to," she rushed

on before he could interrupt. "I give you credit for that. You never *said* much of anything. It was just the way you said the few pleasantries you threw me, like some people throw a useless bone to a dog. It was just what I thought I read in your eyes when you looked down into mine. The way you held my hand; the tingles that went up and down me when you touched me. Just the nearness of you in the same room used to make me feel different— like I was being uplifted out of the muck of my profession. Like . . . Well, skip it Bill." The long yellow lashes fell across her lovely eyes and she stared at the floor while her head drooped a little forward as though she scanned the hopelessness of her position. Then her head lifted and she faced him bravely.

"It's all right, Bill," she said it softly, feelingly. "I understand. You've treated me swell. Like a lady. I wish to God I'd known you years ago. I— I might have been different."

Bill saw the moisture in her eyes. They were big and wide and dark. He started toward her with some vague impulse of comforting her.

But she waved him off. "I don't want any consolations, Bill. I—I couldn't stand it. Not after—not after the other night. Just let me keep my memories of that, Bill."

She turned at the door and faced him through her tears, one arm extended as though to ward him off. "Please don't, Bill. I'll—I'll be all right.

Congratulations to—to you and Marcia. I don't know if it's acceptable from me, but I'm—I'm wishing you both all the luck. Good-bye, Bill."

For a long time after Lola had gone Bill stood there by the desk, his troubled glance vindictively upon the floor. What had he done? What had he said the other night to have made her feel like that? How could he have been such a fool as to have raised her hopes that way? How . . . ?

Carefully, step by step as well as he could, he retraced in his mind the events of that fateful night when he had walked with her beyond the edge of town.

He'd met her that night while making a round of the resorts with Tranter. She had come walking along the street through the crowds of hell-raising merry-makers. He'd suggested they take in the sights. She had seemed a bit reluctant, but had let him hold her hand. He couldn't see now why he had even wanted to hold her hand; he must have been kind of daffy in the head that night. Moonstruck, maybe. They had walked along in silence for a spell, not heading in any special direction, but sort of gravitating toward the edge of town. Bill couldn't remember now whether it had been he or she who had pointed their steps in that direction, but if it had been he, he decided grimly, he had ought to have been shot! After all, he was in love with Marcia Globe. Why in the devil had he ever suggested going for a walk with Lola? "It just goes to show," he muttered, "the crazy things a gent'll sometimes do when his mind's on somethin' else. If Marcia ever hears of this, she'll prob'ly nail my hide to the fence an' fill it full o' buck-shot! Don't know's I'd blame her much, at that."

It didn't seem noways possible that a grown man could be so foolish—yet there it was. He sure had been! It looked like some gent's just had the Devil's own luck at getting into scrapes—out of one and into another!

Lola, after leaving Bill, quickly dried her tears, and the glint of a heady anger drove considerable of the loveliness from her jade-green eyes. She struck out across the road with a vicious swing of the hips, her determined stride swiftly eating up the interval between the Sheriff's Office and the Broken Harp saloon of Emanuel Venta.

There were not many patrons still inside when she pushed through the swinging doors. But Venta was there, as usual, behind the bar, and he greeted her with an unctuous smirk.

With a beckoning jerk of the head, that shook her golden curls, Lola headed straight for Venta's rear room and living quarters. It was a squalid, depressing place, but Lola was in neither the mood nor the interest to lavish attention upon unimportant trifles. Grabbing a dirty pillow off the rumpled bed, she mopped it across a chair and threw it aside. Sitting down she looked at the still-grinning Venta closely.

Her lips curled with contempt and loathing. "What in hell strikes you as being so funny?" she demanded coldly.

Venta's wiry form drew back a pace before the look that was in her eyes. But he did not lose his oily grin. "Yore man, he ees on the run," he chuckled. "Thees fella Dorne, she's pin the deadwood on heem."

"What are you talking about? Talk English, won't you? Who are you callin' 'my man'?"

"Pecos Borst," said Venta, and showed surprise. "Is eet not so?"

"Borst's a fool," she snapped. "I've broken with him. I'm on my own, now. An' I've got money," she added with soft suggestiveness. "Plenty dinero." She watched the glitter come into his little eyes and her red lips curled again.

"I've got a throat that's needing cutting. Are you up to it?"

"Carramba!" Venta muttered. "Whose throat is thees you are talk about, eh? Borst's? For all the dinero in thees lousy town I would not fool weeth that one." And he made fervent haste to cross himself.

"Pah!" Lola sneered, lighting a tailor-made cigarette and inhaling deeply. "I thought you said Borst was through."

"Well . . ." Venta shrugged. "It ees possible I am

make the mistake, señorita. Señor Borst, he has the w'at-you-call 'long arm'."

"You can forget him. It isn't his throat I'm talking about," she said shortly. "Do you know, or did you ever hear of a fellow who calls himself Tumbleweed?"

Venta shook his head dubiously.

"It makes no difference. He's the one I'm talking about. He fancies he's in love with me. In fact, it's his notion that I've fallen for him. Well, I ain't. He's apt to gum things up—I've got a deal on that's goin' to be profitable if it's worked right. And I mean to see that it is." She studied Venta appraisingly. "Now look," she said confidentially. "You stop this Tumbleweed hombre's clock an' I'll sweeten your pocket to the extent of five hundred dollars—"

"One moment, señorita," Venta held up a hand. "Who ees thees guy, Bumblesneed?"

"Tumbleweed," Lola corrected. "He fancies himself something of a gun thrower. But you needn't worry about him. I saw him shoot. He aimed at a fellow not twenty feet away—and dropped the gent beside him! He couldn't hit the broad side of a barn door. And, anyway, if you're scared, there's nothin' to stop you from bushwhacking him, is there?"

"Seex hondred dollars."

"What do you take me for? Do I look like a walkin' gold mine?"

"You said you got dinero," Venta reminded. "Thees job, she's wort' seex hondred. Take eet or leave eet."

Lola counted out the money. "He'll probably be in town to-night. He's puttin' up a show of workin' for the Sheriff. He'll be in by daylight, sure. Your job's to see that he don't get out again. And," she finished grimly, "I'll be back after the balance of this money if you don't stop him permanent."

He watched the swing of her lithe figure as she moved to the door. But at the door she turned. "What," she asked casually, "would you say would be the proper time to call upon a lady?"

Venta blinked and stared at her curiously. "You goin' to keel a lady, too?"

"Don't be a fool! There's other ways of skinnin' a cat. What time?"

Venta scratched the black bristle that covered his head. "Mebbeso one hour after siesta, I'm think."

With a swish of her short silk skirt Lola wheeled and took her departure.

XVIII / *STARTLING DISCLOSURES*

Bill was still there, dozing at his desk, when Buck Tranter—refreshed with a shave and a good breakfast—arrived at seven o'clock with the bright sunshine pushing the long blue shadows across the warming range.

"Top o' the mornin'," Tranter grinned, getting out his evil-smelling pipe and packing it with tobacco from the sack he had dexterously lifted from Dorne's shirt pocket. "Got the troubles of Spavined Nag all ironed out?"

"Gents with beamin' faces don't agree with me before breakfast," Dorne growled, sitting up to yawn and stretch. "Cripes—who'd want to be a sheriff? I wish to hell I'd stuck to ranchin' like a civilized gent had ought to! This hazin' of other folks' problems is no sinecure. By gosh, I got troubles enough of my own."

"You shore look it," Tranter said, with a vast disregard of tact. "What did that Lola skirt want around here last night? I seen her leavin'."

"She wanted," Bill said, scowling, "to warn me against hirin' nosey squirts like you."

"I wouldn't be surprised," said Tranter, puffing complacently. "She knows I got her number. It's a funny thing, Bill, but human naichure's like that—if a fella does somebody a meanness what somebody else know about, he shore takes on a hate for the second somebody which, if it could be harnessed like a waterfall, would run all the dang mills in this yere country."

Bill stared at him grimly. Then, wheeling, he snapped: "Quit blowin' that dang smoke at me! Makes me smell like a ol' rotten cabbage!"

"Wal," Tranter grunted, "if yuh'd sit down fer a spell 'stead o' waltzin' round like a hen on a hot griddle, this yere smoke would be able tuh git out the door."

"Aw—make a noise like a hoop an' roll away!"

Tranter looked him over curiously. "Seems like you're cloudin' up fer a squall. I'm allowin' you'll rare plumb outen yore trousers when yuh hear the latest."

Bill whirled. "What's happened now?"

"Bill, a fella was killed las' night—early this mornin' rather. 'There was a knife stuffed dang near out o' sight in his gullet!"

"Who?" There was impatience as well as irritation in Bill's single word.

"Guy that used tuh run the Broken Harp—Venta."

"Venta!" Bill snarled. "Who'd wanta knife that fool?"

"I don't know who'd wanta—but some gent sure did. Or," Tranter added thoughtfully, "mebbe it was a female. I seen that Lola dame tramp into Venta's place this mawnin'. It was right after she left here." And there was speculation in the glance he flipped at Dorne.

"Don't act no dumber than Nature made you. Why should Lola want Venta out of the way?"

"Couldn't say," Tranter shrugged. "That's yore problem—if yuh're int'rested." He smoked a moment in silence, then added, "She sure as hell went into the Broken Harp when she left you. Why should she go there, anyhow, since we're askin' questions?"

Bill had no answer for that. He would like to know himself.

"That skirt," Tranter offered, "is pow'ful easy on the eyes. But them's the kind that gits a gent in trouble. I've sweated 'round cowhands long enough tuh know that yuh can't never tell what fool thing'll appeal to a puncher as bein' a reasonable thing tuh do."

"Why," Bill growled, "don't you stick to one subject?"

"I am. The Lola dame."

"She didn't have nothin' to do with Venta's gettin' knifed, so get it out of yore thick head."

"Did she have anythin' tuh do with yore takin' a walk out past the bridge of town the other night?"

Bill swore, glared for a moment and went stamping out of the office. He was so mad and resentful and irritated with Tranter and everything else in general that he almost walked smack into a man heading for the office. He looked up with a muttered apology and saw that the man was Tumbleweed.

"Got some news fer yer," the scar-faced deputy said from the corner of his mouth. "In a hurry?"

"No," Bill grunted and, swinging into step beside him, headed back toward the office.

"Borst," Tumbleweed confided, "didn't know nothin' about them rustled cattle bein' on his range. He was madder'n a hatter when one of the boys brought him word. Swore someone was out ter frame 'im."

Dorne stopped. He looked at Tumbleweed closely. "You sure of that?"

"Wal, I was there when the puncher brung the word."

Tumbleweed's seamed and sun-darkened countenance looked serious and candid. Dorne could not doubt that the man spoke the truth. This was putting things in a muddle, right, he thought. Surely no one else in this country would be loco enough to slap that Hashknife brand on other folk's cattle. And yet, if Tumbleweed had been on hand when the news had been brought Borst—

Shucks, he reflected. Tumbleweed might be speaking in good faith, and yet be mistaken. He said, "Well, that certainly puts a different complexion on a couple of things."

"I figgered it would; thought yer'd be wantin' ter know," Tumbleweed nodded. "An' by the way, a fella was stabbed here in town this mornin'. That guy what runs the Broken Harp. He—"

"I know about that," Bill growled. "I gotta go see about a inquest on him."

"Inquest?" Tumbleweed's voice had not raised much, but it had raised. "I didn't know the law held a inquest on a gent unless he was daid."

Dorne looked at him curiously as they resumed their way toward the office. When they reached the steps, Bill said, "It don't."

"But," muttered Tumbleweed as they stepped inside, "that fella ain't daid."

"Wal, he never admitted it, mebbe," Tranter grunted, "but we planted 'im jest the same."

Dorne looked from Tumbleweed to Tranter and back again. There was a startled expression on Tumbleweed's face. A sardonic leer curled Tranter's saturnine lips.

Tumbleweed snarled "Well, he wasn't—" and closed his mouth tightly on the rest.

"Says which?" Tranter grinned. "Don't be modest, now. Let's hear the rest o' that thought yuh was fittin' wings to."

But Tumbleweed stood there, morose and silent—alert.

Dorne said, "Tranter, what the hell did you want to bury that bird for before we held an inquest? Now he'll have to be dug up again!"

"What for? He was killed by a knife-wound, wa'n't he? What more do yuh hev tuh know?"

"We have to find out who killed him, of course. We—"

"Well, no inquest is gonna tell yuh that!"

Dorne smothered an oath. "Tumble tells me that Borst didn't know there was rustled cattle on his range—"

"Tumble tells a heap o' things besides his beads," Tranter snorted, and eyed his brother deputy with open contempt.

"Listen, you!" Tumbleweed growled. "Don't ride me too far less'n yer anxious ter step inter smoke!"

"Hell, you couldn't fog a winder pane in a thirty-below freeze!"

Dorne said, "Cut the wranglin' or I'll knock yore heads together. This is a sheriff's office an' what we're discussin' is serious business."

"Then you better git some other hombre in place of this polecat Tranter," Tumbleweed said wickedly. "He's the bird that drove them stolen beeves onto Borst's range! I lay out on the rimrock an' watched him do it!"

Dorne whirled on Tranter with an oath.

"The skinny wart is right," Tranter chuckled, looking Bill squarely in the eye. "Fer onct he told the truth."

"You drove that rustled stock on Borst's range!" Dorne blazed. "What in hell did you think you was doin'? By cripes, I got a notion—"

"Save it then," Tranter sneered. "I drove them beeves onto Borst's range because they had Borst's brand on 'em—fresh over their original marks. Borst had 'em cached in a box-cañon what had a pole fence built across the open end. They was goin' onto his range, anyhow, eventually. What do yuh s'pose he had his waddies out there rebrandin' 'em for? I jest hazed 'em into the open a mite arly, is all, workin' on the theory 'eventually-why-not-now.' An' if this little sidewinder saw me do it, he must be in with Borst, 'cause that cañon was plumb concealed to the average eye an' the chances of him stumblin' acrost it by accident is plumb remote."

"You found it!" Tumbleweed snarled.

"Sure I found it. I was lookin' fer it, an' I'm a gent what knows his way around. I guess you was lookin' fer it, too!"

"Yeah. *AN' I WAS LOOKIN' WHEN YOU WAS HEATIN' UP YER BRANDIN' IRON!*"

"Why, yuh lousy, lyin' sidewinder!" Tranter's gun was in his hand and the hammer was nearly full back when Dorne grabbed his wrist and forced the gun's muzzle toward the floor. Tranter abruptly yielded to superior opinion and relinquished the weapon. Bill put it on the desk out of reach.

"I don't know which of you birds to believe," he growled. "But one of you's lyin' sure. Question is, which?" And his cold stare went from one to the other angrily.

"Better can us both," Tranter suggested. "Then you'll have the double-crosser where he can't get into mischief fer a while."

Tumbleweed just glowered.

Bill said, "Tumble, you go on back to the Hashknife an' keep yore eyes peeled for a chance to rejoin Borst, if he's still in the country an' comes back to his spread for anythin'. I'll see you out there Monday afternoon. We're confiscatin' that property an' are goin' to auction it off at a Sheriff's sale. If Borst comes back, you stick with him till you find a chance to get me word of his whereabouts without him gettin' suspicious. Get goin' before you an' Tranter get to throwin' lead."

And, as Tumbleweed started for the door, Bill said to Tranter, "You come along with me. I'm goin' to look into this Venta killin'. An' I better not find you did it because he had it comin' to him and would have got it anyway sooner or later!"

Tranter's scowl dissolved into a sheepish grin. "I thought that was a cute trick I played on Borst. After all, the big lobo was havin' his men rebrand 'em. They was stolen critters. They—"

"Skip it," Bill said curtly. "I heard enough about them steers."

From the coroner, Bill learned that what Tranter had told him about Venta's stabbing was true. There was one knife thrust, or rather, wound, in Venta's body, the coroner said. No other marks of violence. And the knife had been in the wound when he and Tranter, summoned by one of the Broken Harp bartenders, had first examined him.

Bill thanked him and, followed by Tranter, turned his steps toward the Broken Harp. At this time in the morning no one was in the place save a sleepy-eyed barman and a slow-motion swamper.

Bill eyed the bartender coldly. "You the bird that found Venta?"

The barman nodded surlily.

"What time?"

" 'Bout 4 o'clock this mornin'."

"Where?"

"In the back room."

"Elucidate," Bill snapped. "Where was he layin'? Or wasn't he?"

"He was layin' on his back with a knife stickin' out of his chest an' blood all over," the bartender said uneasily, his shifty glance travelling from Bill to Tranter and back again. "Yuh needn't look at me like that," he blurted. "*I* didn't kill 'im!"

"Nobody's accusin' you of killin' him. Who was in the room with him?"

"A skinny gent with a knife-scar along the left side of his face from chin to ear. I seen him around before, once or twicet. But I don't know who he is. Some stranger. He's got a mean look an' a pair of pale eyes that are enough to give a gent the creeps."

"Tumbleweed—sure as I been weaned a week!" Tranter ejaculated joyously. "I tol yuh that scorpion was a wrong 'un! I can spot 'em every time! Wisht tuh heck I could recollect where I seen his mug before."

Bill Dorne's face was a study. It was hard for him to believe that Tumbleweed could have stabbed Venta. Yet the implication was plain as the nose on Tranter's face.

"But Tumble's a trigger man," Bill muttered weakly.

"He's a guy which uses whatever's handiest at the time he wants tuh use it," Tranter said emphatically. "You slipped, Bill, when yuh made that bird a depity. Why don'tcha admit it? The guy's crooked as a dawg's hind laig!"

But Bill was loyal. "I gotta see it proved," he declared. "I'm bettin' Tumble will have a explanation—"

"Sure he will! He'd be a fool if he didn't," Tranter scoffed. "An' whatever else he is he ain't no fool. Why don't yuh look up his references? Why don't yuh drop a line tuh them places where he says he's worked? Find out what they know about him. Cripes, fer all you know, he mebbe murdered the las' guy he worked for an'—"

"Why don't you give that imagination of yores a rest?" Bill growled irritably. "You'll be wearin' the damn' thing out!" He swung his fighter's broad tapering shoulders toward the bartender squarely. "How long was this fella back there with Venta? You remember?"

"'Bout ten minutes—mebbe less."

"How do you place the time so close?"

"Well," the fellow rasped his chin, looked at Bill uncertainly, blinked and shifted his feet uneasily. His mouth was partly open, but he didn't look as though he contemplated saying any more.

Bill's narrowed eyes took on a steely glint. He took a forward step with a grimness that drove the other back. "You talk, by gosh, or I'll scatter yore dad-blamed teeth all over this place!"

"But—but," the man stammered, "if I say what I got in my mind you'll be apt to put the wrong interp—"

"You say it an' let me be the judge of the way to take it," Bill grunted coldly. "How did you fix that time so accurate?"

"You're askin' fer it," the bartender said. "I know this hombre was in the back room with Venta because jest after they went back there a dame come in here lookin' for Venta, an'—"

"What dame?"

"Lola—the gal that used to work for Borst."

XIX / VILLAINY AFOOT

Bill Dorne's pugnacious underlip thrust grimly forward in the drive of his rising passion. The gathering violence in him could be seen definitely in the bulging muscle along his jaw and the tautness of the cords in his flushing neck.

The bartender gave back a few uncertain steps, paling visibly, one hand lifted before him as though to ward off an expected blow.

And, indeed, Bill's expression gave cause for such alarm. Bill snarled, "I got no special interest in Lola; get that straight. *But*—I don't never stand by an' twiddle my fingers when a good woman's name is slandered, be she a dance hall girl, a waitress or the President's wife! *Get me?*"

"Nobody's slanderin' her," the barman said with shaking lips. "An' if it sounded like a slur to you, I'm apologizin'. No slur was meant."

Most of the anger washed from Bill's cheeks and a cold contempt replaced it. "You sure crawfish graceful," he drawled scathingly.

"You didn't give me time to finish what I was tellin' yuh when you jumped me," the barman protested. "Hell, Sheriff, I wasn't figurin' to slander Lola. Nor any other girl. I was tellin' you about Venta—"

"Well, get on with it," Bill growled coldly.

"I fixed the time," the man resumed with a faint

tinge of resentment colouring the pallor of his face, "on account of Lola comin' in right after him an' likewise wantin' to habla with Venta. She seemed some impatient. Kept pacin' the floor like she had somethin' on her mind. An' I reckon she did have. 'Cause after eight or ten minutes, she mutters somethin' under her breath and starts fer the door of that there back room," and he flung his arm out toward it in a dramatic gesture that would have done credit to a first-rate Shakespearean.

Bill and Tranter looking duly impressed, he went on:

"I says, 'Yuh better not go in there till that other gent comes out. Venta give me orders he wasn't to be interrupted.' But she gives me a sour look an' keeps right on waltzin' towards the back room. 'My business,' she says, 'is jest as important as anybody's. I want to see Venta pronto—an' I'm goin' to.'

"She grabs the handle an' yanks the door open real determined, an' goes on inside—"

Bill growled, "How many people was in here when she done all this?"

"Nobody," the barman said, "'ceptin' me an' her. Venta had thrown the last drunk out half an hour before. He was closin' up for the night."

"I told him to close this joint at two," Bill drawled. "If he'd 'a' done it he'd be alive this minute instead of bein' six feet under the sod."

The barman nodded. "I reckon there ain't no

doubt about that. It goes to show that it's a heap healthier to obey the law," he said, and scowled at Tranter's sardonic grin. "Well, to git on with the story—Lola opens the door to Venta's private room an' goes on in. Seems like I heard a start, but I couldn't swear to it. Anyhow, a coupla moments later she lets out a squawk an' comes outa there like she'd seen a ghost. Cripes, her face was whiter'n a frog's belly!"

He paused to be sure his audience was getting the full measure of appreciation from his oratory. Then he said in an awful whisper, "She tells me Venta's sprawled on his back inside there with a knife buried in his guts!"

"It was in his chest," Tranter said.

The barman scowled. "Who's tellin' this story? You, or me? . . . Well, then, let me tell it. *She* said it was buried in his guts!"

"What did you do?" Bill asked.

"I took a look an' sure enough it was like she said, only the knife was in his chest," he shot a scowl at Tranter. "Soon's I saw what was up, I dashed out into the street, figgerin' to rush for yore office. But there was Tranter goin' by, so I yells at him an' he sent me to get the coroner."

Bill looked at Tranter. "Where's the knife?"

"Coroner's got it," Tranter grunted, and getting out his battered pipe, lifted the barman's sack of Durham and filled the blackened bowl.

The barman kept his mouth shut, but his looks

were plenty significant. They became more so when Tranter put the sack in his pants pocket and, lighting his pipe, went strolling toward the batwing doors.

"Thanks," Bill muttered, and followed Tranter out.

On their way back toward the Sheriff's Office, Bill said, "This sure is a mess."

"A helluva situation an' no mistake," Tranter agreed equably. "You goin' to write them letters?"

"What letters?"

"Them letters to the Box O B an' Deer Lodge—where Tumbleweed, the damn' liar, says he used to work."

"Well, it's an idea," Bill admitted. "Mebbe I better wire them places. If Tumble's crooked, like you think, the sooner we find it out the better for all concerned."

"Yeah—the better fer us, anyhow. Let's go wire 'em now."

The wires sent, with a request for speedy answers, Bill said to Tranter,

"Tell you what, Buck. This is a durn good time to hunt up them Wineglass two-year-olds that was rustled three-four days ago. Let's get our hawsses."

"Where you figgerin' tuh hunt?"

"Thought we might cull through some of that rustled stock you drove onto Borst's range the night before last. That was a dumb stunt you pulled. If you'd left the critters where you found 'em an' come in an' told me, we could have nailed his hide—"

"We could of et beans, too," Tranter scoffed. "D'you think with that scurvy Tumbleweed atop the rimrock, they'd have been there when we got back?"

"But you didn't know he was up there."

"The hell I didn't! I didn't know it was *him*—but I knew someone was there. I seen the glint of his rifle. I was expectin' the bite of its lead, too, I can tell you. I had a bad few minutes gettin' them critters outen that dang box-cañon. An' a lot of thanks I got fer doin' it!"

"Did you expect me to kiss you?" Dorne snorted.

"Well, I've been kissed by better lookin' speciments than you! C'mon, le's get the nags an' be on our way before I git mad an' tell yuh where tuh stuff this job."

"Hoot Owl" Polsky, Globe's Wineglass foreman, dismounted in a shallow draw shaded by cottonwoods and, leaving his mount on trailing reins where it was concealed by the dusty foliage, placed his back against a cottonwood's bole and rolled himself a brown-paper cigarette.

The golden ball of Apollo had long since dipped behind the serrated crests of the purple western mountains when at last Polsky, looking across the miles of yellow earth, beheld a horseman cantering out upon the trail from the distant pass.

Polsky heaved a sigh, pinched out his cigarette and stowed the butt carefully in his pocket. Then he got to his feet and stretched. He would soon be getting back to the outfit. The cook would likely do a tolerable amount of grumbling, but would eventually produce a tardy supper for him. Polsky heaved another sigh and smacked his lips in anticipation. Riding the Spavined Nag Range was one sure way of working up an appetite, he reflected.

He could hear the distant horse's hoofs now, faintly. In a few minutes the rider would enter this draw. Polsky loosened his gunbelt a notch so that it would sag his holster at a handier angle. He examined his gun to make sure the mechanism was free of grit. When he shoved the weapon back in its sheath, his features looked as smoothly inscrutable as those of a Chinese gambler.

Five minutes later Tumbleweed dismounted in the cottonwood grove and nodded to Polsky curtly. There was no sign of his usual slurred dialect when he spoke; his words were clipped and terse:

"What did you find out?"

"The bulk of the Wineglass' marketable beef will be held to-night at Keystone Cañon and a heavy guard set over 'em to make sure they ain't got away with by Borst's rustlers," Polsky said, and watched the other alertly.

"Have you contacted Krayson or Harniss?"

"No. I couldn't get at 'em. They've definitely swung to Borst."

Tumbleweed scowled, then shrugged. "All right. Let 'em go. Where's Globe?"

Polsky eyed Tumbleweed curiously; but nothing was to be read from that ugly, sneering countenance. Nothing ever had, Polsky reflected bitterly. It was no cinch, he thought, working for a man who kept a fellow as much in the dark as Tumbleweed kept him. Who was this Tumbleweed hombre? It was a thing he'd often wondered in the last eight months since Tumbleweed had contacted him and offered to get him a job as foreman on the Wineglass outfit, in exchange for a little information occasionally. It struck Polsky now as he looked at his companion, that he would not have to go far to put his hand on the brains of Borst's rustling gang.

He was wrong, but he never found it out.

"Where's Globe?" Tumbleweed repeated.

"In town—but he sent out word he'd be at the ranch to-night." Polksy ran his tongue across his lips, squared his shoulders in such a way that his hand, hooked in his gunbelt, was close to his holstered weapon. Then he said suggestively, "Be interestin' to know what you've got on Globe. Or against him."

"Do you think so?" Tumbleweed's voice was

soft, and the knife-scar that ran from chin to ear along the left side of his face began to glow.

But Polsky had figured his chances and was determined to carry his plan through. He had never seen Tumbleweed draw, but he had a pretty good notion that Tumbleweed was two-thirds bluff and the other third hard looks. But he wasn't taking any chances; his hand was so close to his gun that he could flip it free of leather with a single flick of the wrist. And he aimed to do so if Tumbleweed gave indication that he was going to act up.

"Think so?" he jeered. "Hell—I *know* so! In fact, fella, I know enough about yore game to know I'm bein' damn well took advantage of. I want more money. In the future an' for the past. An' I'm wantin' my back pay right damn now!"

"Shucks," Tumbleweed murmured easily. "You don't need no money."

"You think not?"

"No," Tumbleweed grinned: "They don't use money where you're goin'," and shot him through the heart.

There was a hunted, haunted light in Lola's jade-green eyes as she walked toward Globe's town residence through the blazing heat of the midday sun. The air was scorching, breathless, yet she did not seem to notice. Nor did she feel the blistering heat of the sand as she crossed the road to avoid a group of freighters who were unloading barrels of whisky before the Black Bottle Bar. Her mind was absorbed with a scene she could not thrust from her memory—the picture of Venta writhing and groaning on the floor, and of herself bending over him and thrusting home that knife protruding from his chest, and of the spurting blood and the awful terror in his eyes. But the eyes and the blood were far the worst; she could see the bulging whites of them now—they had followed her all morning, no matter where she went or what she did. Not for an instant had they vanished, and their curse was just as potent now as when she'd driven home that blade. And the blood—Gawd! she could feel it on her fingers now!

Why had she ever touched that blade? Why had she ever let herself kill that murdering bravo? Why—

But she knew. She had seen him lying there and the thought had flashed through her instantly that he had failed in the task she set for him. He had been alive, though—conscious! If he hadn't talked already, he would as soon as he got . . . And then some tiny inner voice had whispered—"Kill him, you fool! Dead men do not talk! Tumbleweed can wring no confession from a stiff!" And she stooped and thrust the knife in deep and turned it. *Ugh!* That blood! And the curse in those bulging, dying eyes!

She hurried her steps unconsciously, keeping pace with her turbulent thoughts. Her fear of

Venta talking had been born of panic. She realized it now. If Venta had intended talking he must have talked before she'd found him. He'd been dying then. She'd been a fool to put her hand to steel already buried!

And even if he'd lasted long enough to tell the law how he'd come to such an untimely end, who would have believed him? Not Dorne, surely! Dorne was not even aware she was acquainted with Tumbleweed. Dorne could have found no motive, no incentive for her to have hired a man to do away with Tumbleweed.

"Damn Tumbleweed!" she muttered, and cursed the night their paths had crossed.

She could not think how Tumbleweed had conceived of Venta's intention in time to turn the tables as he had done so neatly. Venta must have blundered.

She looked up to see the Globe gate in front of her. By sheer willpower she composed her features, unlatched the gate and walked to the veranda, went up the steps and knocked with a steady hand upon the door. The same hand from which this morning she had scrubbed the sticky blood. It had been pure luck, she thought, that the pale-faced bartender had not noticed that reddened hand.

From the interior of the house she could hear light footsteps coming toward the door. And then Marcia stood there before her. The delicate, pretty features of the Mayor's daughter reflected wonder and curiosity as she realized her visitor's identity.

"Could I come in a moment?" Lola asked in a husky voice that seemed to catch deep down in rounded ivory throat. "I—it's—it's about the Sheriff. About Bill Dorne. I—I just had to see you. I—I knew you'd understand."

Wonderingly, a trifle frightened, too, Marcia held open the door.

XX / "ON THE ORDERS OF PECOS BORST!"

"Well," said Tranter, as he and Dorne turned their horses' heads toward town, "that's shore that."

"It sure is," Dorne said, turning up his collar against the chill wind sweeping up off the range now that the sun was down. "It most usually is, in fact. We've got Pecos Borst dead to rights. There's only one thing, now we've found Globe's missin' two-year-olds with the Hashknife brand blotched over the Wineglass, that could be a bigger card to our hand. An' that's for you or me to see Friend Pecos with a runnin' iron in hand kneelin' over a tied-up dogie."

"Some gents," said Tranter drily, "wouldn't be satisfied with a castle, less'n they had a picket fence built roun' it—an' then they'd prob'ly yowl about the colour of the paint!"

Bill snorted.

"What kinda knife was that blade that was used to boost Venta into the Happy Hunting Grounds?"

"Jest a ord'nary bone-handled bowie. Won't do yuh no good tuh look at it. Looks jest the same as forty thousan' others. Every sheep herder an' his brother totes one of 'em. Some Mexicans I've met, packs two. Down in Arkansaw they make 'em out of ol' rasps. They're wicked weapons, all right, but dang few of 'em has distinguishin' marks. This one shore ain't anyhow."

"Gettin' back to the matter of Venta's death," Dorne cut in, "why do you reckon the fella used a Arkansas toothpick on him? Reckon he had some special reason?"

"I opine he figgered to use the first thin' he clapped hand to," Tranter said. "Or else he heard the ol' saw 'bout silence bein' golden an'—" He broke off to eye Bill searchingly. "Yuh know, the more I think about it, the more I'm inclined tuh place my bets on either that skinny Tumbleweed jasper or that Lola skirt as bein' the most likely candidate for—"

"Leave the girl out of it," Bill growled brusquely. "She couldn't have no motive. And as for Tumble—"

"*Say!*" Tranter broke in wide-eyed. "I jest recollected where I seen that skinny gopher before! I was pawin' through that drawer of ol' reward notices in yore desk the other day. There's a picture in there what fits that pelican's like a glove! Cripes, you wait an' see! Them places yuh wired won't know a thing about 'im!"

Tranter was wrong—but not very.

Lola, from her seat in Mayor Frank Globe's most comfortable rocker, eyed Marcia where she stood beside the centre table with one hand caught to her breast and the other holding to the edge of the table as though for support. Why, Lola wondered contemptuously, should Bill Dorne prefer this girl instead of herself? What had Marcia Globe to offer a man like Bill that she had not?

Looks? To be sure, Marcia was pretty in a dark, brunette way, Lola admitted grudgingly. She seemed very feminine with her dark black hair tied in a loose knot back of her neck, and her gingham dress and her eyes—deep brown pools these latter were. But her nose! Lola's red lips curled. What man would be fool enough to prefer a snub nose, with freckles marching across its bridge, to a straight and slender patrician affair like her own? No, she decided, it couldn't be looks, for she knew—her glass had told her many times—that she was far the better looking of the two.

What was it then? Was it because Marcia was the Mayor's daughter while she was the ex–faro dealer of Borst's late Gloden Stack? Could *that* be it? Little fires sprang up in the depths of her jade-green eyes. But she quickly veiled them with her lashes. This little fool might have a bit more perception than one would think. It was best to take no chances.

Lola hid her hate behind a mask of sadness, a mask displaying shame and humiliation and other things less easily definable, as well. Her voice came huskily when she spoke and there was a moist brightness to her eyes that surely, she thought, the little fool could see.

Marcia did see. "Why you're crying!" she said, drawing closer with a ready sympathy. She knew the sort of woman Lola was—one could hardly help it in a town of this size. But she stifled her natural repugnance in the fullness of her generosity. Lola was a girl in trouble; she had come to her for help, perhaps advice. She must be looking on Marcia as a possible Good Samaritan—or beacon light shining whitely through this wilderness of sin.

Marcia's thoughts were growing complex. She shook free of them. This woman was here for help or guidance. And she should have it, if it lay within Marcia's power to help.

Her arms went round Lola comfortingly, reassuringly, protectingly, as she knelt beside her on the carpeted floor. "You poor girl," Marcia's words were soft with sympathy. "You poor, poor girl. Will it make things easier for you if you tell me about it? Maybe I can help. Maybe—"

"Oh, you don't know, Miss!" Lola said burying her face against Marcia's shoulder, and allowing her own shoulders to shake convulsively. She was a good actress and she knew her part and lines. She proved it when she raised a tear-stained face to Marcia's and moaned. "You think I'm a bad woman—Oh, I know you do! You think I live in sin and—Oh, you'll never believe me when I say I've always been good, even if I never had a decent chance in life. You won't believe me when

I tell you that I never let a—that I never did a—that—that—" she floundered hopelessly, gulped, and bravely finished, "That I'm going to have a baby and it's not my fault." And she looked at Marcia piteously, with her lovely eyes all blurred and red.

Marcia looked a little shocked, but she was all compassion, sympathy. She hugged Lola to her closely and sort of rocked her as a mother might a sick or frightened child. She spoke soft soothing words until the paroxysms and the sobs that came from Lola ceased.

She patted Lola's shoulder and cried a bit herself.

But presently Lola wailed, albeit softly, "Oh, what shall I do? What *can* I do? How will I ever hold up my head again?"

"Now," whispered Marcia soothingly, "everything will come out all right. All things happen for the best; believe it. God is just—"

"No he isn't!" Lola panted fiercely, between her tears. "What did I ever do to deserve this? *I,* who always lived by the Golden Rule and never harmed anybody? Why, do you know—that lousy Borst flung me out of his place before Bill—before Sheriff Dorne burned it down because I wouldn't use marked cards to cheat people out of their hard-earned money! Threw me out like an old shoe! And knowing I couldn't get a job and was going to have a—"

"Did—is—is the baby his?" Marcia stammered hastily, her cheeks scarlet.

"No," Lola said emphatically. Then huskily, "But I'll never tell who its father is—I never will! If Bill don't want—Oh!" she caught a hand to her lips and looked at Marcia wildly.

She had not needed to worry about Marcia's perceptions. She knew it now when she felt Marcia's form grow stiff and saw the startled pallor that washed the colour from Marcia's cheeks and widened her eyes incredulously. She felt Marcia's fingers digging into her arms cruelly. "Did—you say 'Bill'?"

"I won't tell!" Lola sobbed. "I won't! I won't! You've got no right to ask me things like that!"

"If you're talking about—" Marcia bit the disloyal words off swiftly. But there was a light of determination in the brown glance she sent to Lola's face. "You'll have to tell me who this man is," she said quietly, insistently. "I've got to know. I've got a special reason for wanting to know. I—"

"Well, I ain't going to tell you!" Lola flashed. "Don't you think I've got some pride? Just because I've worked in a gambling dive, you needn't think I—"

"Tell me!" Marcia was firm. "I'll help you all I can, but you've got to tell me this Bill's full name. Can't you see you've got to? How can I help you unless you tell me—"

"I ain't going to!" Lola said doggedly. "I—I guess I came to the wrong place after all. I might have known—" she let the sentence trail off and made as though to rise. But Marcia was too quick for her, as Lola hoped she'd be.

"No," Marcia said. "You're not going until you tell me that man's last name. Bill what?"

"Bill Dorne—if you've got to know!" Lola flared with curling lips. "I hate him! I don't know why I should protect his good name; he didn't give a damn about mine! Bill Dorne—that's who he is!"

Marcia slowly, automatically, straightened to her feet. Her cheeks had gone deathly pale and all the light and laughter that had been in her when she had answered the door to Lola's knock was gone from her. There was a dead, vacant look to her eyes and she shivered slightly as she stood there with her hands at her breast.

"Bill Dorne," she whispered huskily. "My Bill!"

She was looking at Lola, but she did not seem to see her. She seemed to be seeing something crumble and wither inside her soul.

Looking at her, Lola felt a moment of remorse. But she stifled it instantly at the thought of Bill. Bill was *her* man; she wanted him and she was going to have him—cost what it might to others!

She got to her feet, remembering that she must not forget her role. She looked at Marcia as though uncertainly. "What did you say, Miss?"

"Nothing," Marcia answered dully; "nothing that matters, now. I guess perhaps you were right. You'd better go."

And as Lola tiptoed from the room she heard Marcia sink heavily to a chair and her lips curled contemptuously. "Serves her right, the stuck-up hussy!" she said viciously beneath her breath.

"Where do yuh reckon Mendota an' that gamblin' Phoenix John lit out to?" Tranter asked, as he and Dorne came jogging into town. The dusty road was dappled with bars of light from the open doors and windows, and sounds of Spavined Nag's eternal night life blared from the saloons and honkytonks they passed. "Yuh reckon they've left the country?"

"I hope so," Bill said wearily, "but I doubt it. No such luck. I allow this business will have to be fought out to a finish, Buck. I reckon you was right when you said Borst wasn't the quittin' kind. I've sorta got a hunch we're goin' to be hearin' from him again. I only hope I can get my hands on him before he—"

"Shucks," Tranter cut in, "I allow yuh'll get yore hands on him—eventshully. Course he might stick up the bank again an' two-three other meannesses, but—Say! Ain't that the coroner comin'?"

Tranter's eyes were good, keened no doubt by many a midnight ride along the owl-hoot trail. The coroner was coming toward them out of the shadowy lane that led to his establishment some distance back from the street. There was another man with him, who looked to Bill like Gospel Jones. And so it proved to be.

The coroner and the parson came up to where Dorne and Tranter sat their dusty broncs. The coroner flourished a paper; thrust it triumphantly at Dorne. "I've pegged yore bank-robbers, Bill," he panted. "Got a signed confession—read it!"

"It'll keep," Bill said, and thrust the paper in his pocket. "Who are they?"

"An' how'd yuh git the confeshun?" Tranter echoed.

Gospel Jones cleared his throat. "Well," he said apologetically, "we maybe overstepped our authority a bit, but we led Joe Fuddabaugh to believe his condition had taken a turn for the worse. Fact is, I hinted he was dyin' an' had better make his peace before 'twas too late. He got some scared, what with that brimstone sermon I up an' preached him, an' the coroner here took down his statement."

"Yeah," Dorne growled impatiently, "but who robbed the bank?"

"Him," the coroner squeaked. "Him an' his pardner, Smoky Leupp, on the orders of Pecos Borst, an' aided an' abetted by Banker Fisk!"

XXI / *ACTION!*

Well, Bill reflected sardonically, now he knew. But like most knowlege, when one has it, it didn't do him any considerable amount of good. Joe Fuddabaugh would not busy himself in robbing any more banks for quite some while, for in that gun battle before the burning of the Golden Stack Joe had absorbed a tolerable amount of lead, and Smoky Leupp had quit the business for good.

Giving orders that Joe should be removed to the jail as soon as he had convalesced past the danger point, Bill grunted a "Come on," at Tranter and, kicking his horse in the ribs, moved on down the street in the direction of the telegraph office, an installation of the express company and uncommon handy in these days of turbulence.

"Ain't but one woeful wire come in for the Sheriff's Office," the telegraph operator grinned, when he saw his visitors. "Here y'are Mr. Dorne," he added, and pased Bill a yellow envelope which Bill ripped open pronto, and from which he swiftly extracted a folded yellow paper. Spreading it out, he saw it was the answer to his wire to the Box O B at Salty Crick, Nevada.

NO TUMBLEWEEDS EVER COME ROLLING ONTO THIS SPREAD STOP NOR ANY GENTS ANSWERING YOUR DESCRIPTION

STOP RECKON YOU MUST HAVE THE WRONG OUTFIT OR WRONG SALTY CRICK STOP TRAVIS

Bill read and swore disgustedly. And Tranter, reading over Bill's shoulder, chuckled openly and with apparent gusto. "What'd I tell yuh? I knowed that jasper was crooked soon's I set eyes on 'im!"

The telegraph operator cut Dorne's disgusted snort in two by saying brightly:

"By the way, Sheriff; that wire was sent collect. You owe this office—"

"Never mind," Bill grunted. "You charge it to the county. Bills payable at the end of the month." He broke off as the operator listened to the clacking of his instrument and scrawled hurriedly on a sheet of yellow paper with his left hand. When the instrument quit clicking, he shoved the paper toward Dorne.

"This 'un's paid for. It's from the penitentiary at Deer Lodge."

Bill stared at the note the operator had so hurriedly scribbled; stared again and scowled. "Hell!" he growled, and passed the form to Tranter. Tranter read:

SHERIFF'S OFFICE
SPAVINED NAG ARIZONA:
RE YOUR QUERY STOP DESCRIPTION

FITS NO 875649 TEN SPOT TRULL SENTENCED TO TWENTY YEARS IMPRISONMENT SECOND DEGREE MURDER WIFE STOP TERM STILL HAD FOUR YEARS TO GO WHEN TRULL BROKE JAIL MARCH 16 STOP TRULL STILL AT LARGE STOP CHECK DESCRIPTION REWARD NOTICE OF THAT DATE STOP $2500 REWARD

     ED LATHAM, WARDEN:
     DEER LODGE.

"You rush over to the printer's right away," Bill growled. "Get him to run you off a smear of handbills offerin' 2,500 bucks for capture of Tumbleweed, alias Ten Spot Trull, gambler and gunman, DEAD OR ALIVE! Give 'im Tumble's description an' see that he gits it on in big letters. See that he gets 'em distributed right away an'—"

"Cripes," Tranter interrupted. "He won't distribute 'em or do a dang thing with 'em once he runs 'em off! I can tell yuh that—"

"Don't tell me a thing," Donne snapped curtly. "*I'm* telling *you!* You tell him I got somethin' more important for you to do an' that I'll make it right with him on payday. Also, while you're over there, see that he gets out some notices on Fisk an' Borst, connectin' 'em with that damn bank robbery! *Now git!*"

"What am I supposed to do after that?"

"You come to the Sheriff's Office an' find out!" Bill growled, and headed for that place himself with long ground-eating strides. Over his shoulder he added, "An' take my horse with you. Leave it at the livery with yore own, an' get us a coupla fresh broncs."

"Don't tell me we're goin' tuh do some more damn ridin' at this late hour!" Tranter bellowed.

Dorne strode off without bothering to answer. When a gent worked for the Sheriff's Office, as he himself was finding out, he worked *all* the time! There were no *ifs* or *buts* about it!

Dorne was anxious to take a look at that reward notice mentioned by Tranter as being among that faded pile in his desk drawer. He wondered if it was the same referred to by the Deer Lodge Warden. In an effort to save time, Dorne cut down a dark lane and angled toward a darker alley—the latter running between the Black Bottle Bar and the Cherokee House next door. This alley would lead him to the dusty main street directly across from his office.

His mind was not idle as he strode savagely through the thick murk.

"Workin' for the government!" he snorted, recalling Tumbleweed's statement in connection with Deer Lodge. "I'll say he was—makin' little ones outa big ones, I allow! The dang skunk! An' he used to be a gambler—must've been, with a monicker like that. Murdered his wife, did he?

Tranter sure was right in callin' him a scorpion an' all them other choice adjectives. I could add a few myself!"

Dorne was as much resentful at the manner in which he'd been taken in on his own snap judgement of Tumbleweed as he was at the fact that the fellow was an escaped convict who had murdered his wife. In fact, he was more resentful about the former, being that his code said that a man's personal affairs were his own and the concern of nobody else.

Had he been in a normal state of mind instead of a seething chaos of disconnected thoughts and conjectures, he never would have entered that murky alleyway that ran alongside of Ortega's Black Bottle Bar, knowing as he did the fellow was a minor ally of Borst, and hated the Sheriff on his own account because of Dorne's enforcement of the early closing hour ordinance. But he was too busy with his thoughts just now to give a damn where he was going, just so it got him to the office in the least possible time. There was plenty of work to be done to-night, and now that he had a few leads to follow he was in a high sweat to accomplish a few things.

His mind *did* swing to Marcia Globe for a moment, and he resolved to go and see her at the earliest opportunity. He sure had been neglecting her the last couple of days. "Heck of a way for a prospective bridegroom to be actin'!" he grunted. And just then there was a sibilant *swish!*

Dorne's reflexes were set on a hair-trigger. He ducked instantly, throwing himself sideways toward the window from which that *swish* had come, and the rope's loop that had been meant for his neck slid harmlessly past his drooping shoulders.

He could not see a thing in the black opening of that window, but he reached right in just the same—with both hands. And got himself a grip on something soft and yielding. He grabbed hard, twisted and yanked. He knew he had the wielder of the rope and as he yanked a snarled oath confirmed his knowledge. The next moment he had the sly roper out in the alley. His flailing fists gave the roper no time to reach for a gun, but slammed out hard and fast. Dust rose in ballooning clouds. Grunts and panted oaths from his adversary, who didn't seem to be landing many hard ones, filled the air. But Bill went right on with his work. What he did might best be described as the swiftest, slickest, and most effective and thorough ladling out of justice that Spavined Nag had ever seen ladled! It was a pity, Bill reflected between punches, that a few of the town's tough citizens weren't at hand. But he didn't let that cramp his style. When the fellow sagged, Bill straightened him; when the fellow dropped, Bill picked him up and knocked him down again. When he was through, and he only quit for lack of breath, he got a grip on the fellow's collar and dragged him out of the alley and into the street where the lights from the roaring honkytonks showed that the roper was Señor Ortega himself. Though even his mother would probably have been hard put to have recognized him now.

Bill dragged him to a watering trough and doused his head in three or four times. Ortega eventually came up spluttering. Blood was drooling down his chin, mingling with the water which had brought him to. When he swore Bill saw that he had lost most of his front teeth and that one of his eyes was swollen shut.

"You're a helluva lookin' specimen!" Bill jeered. "I wish to heck I had the chance to put a few more of the hard cases round this burg in the same category! You're goin' to jail—git movin' pronto!"

Ortega was inclined to argue, but a second glance at Bill's cold eyes sent him shuffling along ahead of Bill toward the one place he had never thought to find himself. "By the time you get out," Bill told him, "you'll know better'n to make a pass at another peace officer."

"Peace—hell!" Ortega swore. "Gimme a cyclone any damn time!"

With Ortega safely deposited in the jail, Dorne strode into his office, sat down in the chair behind his desk with a heavy sigh, and pulled open the drawer in which excess reward notices had been dumped by his predecessor. Taking these dusty fliers out he pawed through them swiftly till he found what he wanted.

"Cripes," he grunted, studying the picture below the monetary notice, "that's Tumble, all right. But he sure has changed since he busted outa Deer Lodge! An' he'll change more, when I get my hands on him. What I done to Ortega won't be a patch to what I'll do to that double-crosser! I betcha he was workin' for Borst all the time, damn him!"

The jingle of spur chains, together with the clump of run-down bootheels, announced Tranter's arrival. "Did you get them dodgers?"

Tranter grinned. "Printer's still workin' on 'em. That promise of a little graft on payday sure worked wonders with that fella! He's promised to plaster 'em clear 'crosst the county by mornin'. I dunno how—but he says he'll do it if he has tuh tack 'em up hisself. I got the fresh nags. They're draped tuh the hitch pole outside. Got any more l'l orders yuh wanta git off'n yore chest?"

"Yeah," Bill growled, still studying the picture of Tumbleweed, alias Ten Spot Trull. "Go out an' comb this town for some respectable hellions that're agreeable to posse duty on double pay. Pick a stem-winder to boss 'em, swear 'em in an' send 'em out to get those Wineglass cattle. Then come back here an' I'll have more chores for you."

Tranter clumped out, muttering under his breath.

Bill turned his attention to the small lines of print under Tumbleweed's description. He found that Trull had been convicted of an unpremeditated murderous assault upon his wife when he found she'd been philandering with some neighbouring rancher. It had all happened over in Texas quite a few years ago.

Something clicked in his mind as he digested this information. "Marcia told me once," he muttered, "that she and her stepfather came from Texas. I'd dang near forgotten Ol' Globe wasn't her real father. Now I wonder . . ."

When Tranter returned, Dorne said, "Buck, I got a hunch. Sounds far-fetched as hell, I admit. But I always act on my hunches. This 'un might be like the one I had on Tumbleweed, but I got a notion it ain't."

"What's the hunch?" Tranter asked resignedly. "Somethin' about the location of some more chores fer me?"

"Listen," Bill said. "Listen—Globe came from Texas. Tumbleweed came from Texas. Tumbleweed murdered his wife in a blind rage because he caught her philanderin' with another man. Tumble's wife had a kid girl who vanished about the time Tumble went to the pen. This notice don't say nothin' about the gent Tumble's wife was messin' with, so we can take it for granted that Tumble didn't get a chance to even the score with him."

"So what?"

"Get this," Bill grunted earnestly. "Globe ain't Marcia's real father; he's her stepfather. Buck, I'm bettin' heavy that Globe is the fella that Tumbleweed's wife was sweet on!"

Tranter's eyes bulged as the significance of this sank home. "Cripes!" he muttered. And, "Prancin' prairie chickens!"

"Exactly!" Dorne snapped, surging toward the door. "We gotta warn Globe quick—if it ain't too late already!"

XXII / HELL ALL AROUND

At the ranch headquarters of the Wineglass outfit, lights were burning in both the main house and the bunkhouse. The man who stood in the deep shadows of an alder clump on the low ridge above the buildings could see this clearly. That meant, he decided, that Globe was here, and a faint malignant grin twitched the corners of his mouth. "It's been a long time," he muttered hoarsely, "but by Gawd, we'll clean the slate to-night! That pussy-footin' Lothario's forgotten Teresa's gamblin' husband long ago, I shouldn't wonder. But his memory's due to get a jog when he sees me come walkin' in!" And he glanced downward in the dim light at the black funereal garb of the professional gambler in which he had togged himself for this occasion.

With ugly knife-scarred face alert, muscles taut as coiled spring-steel, the unseen watcher moved stealthily forward, flitting from one patch of shadow to another. The moon was often obscured by scudding clouds, but the man stalking the Wineglass was taking no chances. Too long had he waited for this moment to risk spoiling all by a premature discovery. The man who had waited sixteen years could afford a few extra minutes now, more or less, and was entirely willing to afford them should they make his vengeance the more certain.

Unaware of the menace stalking constantly closer, creeping forward foot by cautious foot, Mayor Frank Globe sat in his ranch house office going over accounts with his manager. "Funny," he said for the tenth time, "where Polsky is."

The manager looked up with a frown. "I can't think what's keeping him," he answered. "He went out on his customary round of inspection this afternoon. He ought to have been back hours ago. Yuh know, Frank, somehow I don't cotton to that jasper. There's too much of the fox about him with his little pointed ears an' his sly, black-button eyes. Frankly, I got a hunch that fella's crooked."

Globe looked at him shrewdly. "I've never seen him, but he came well recommended. He had letters from two big ranchers I used to know in Texas. Both these fellows described him as a hard worker an' a man who knew cows."

"That may be—but it don't prove he ain't a crook. *He* was the one that hired Harniss an' Krayson. An' they sure turned out crookeder than corkscrews."

"What's on your mind?" Globe asked bluntly.

"This. I got a hunch he's in with these rustlers hand-in-glove."

"You think he's on Borst's payroll?"

"If Borst is backin' the rustlers, yes."

"Well—" Globe said, and stopped, his face going the colour of chalk as he lurched mechanically to his feet.

The manager growled, "What the hell?" and turned to follow the direction of Globe's bulging eyes.

Tranter and Bill Dorne reached the door simultaneously, squeezed through and bulged out onto the plank sidewalk and thence into the dust of Spavined Nag's main street. Simultaneously, both men's right hands went to the reins while their lefts grasped the horns of their saddles and their left legs started from the ground for the stirrups. In this position they abruptly froze to the hammering reverberations of pounding hoofs, heard even above the raucous sounds of revelry dinning from the honkytonks which, at this hour, were in full swing.

Across Buck Tranter's tense back Dorne said, "Someody comin' hellity-larrup!"

"Gonna wait?"

"Yeah, we better. No tellin' what's up," Dorne answered and, releasing his grip on the horn, lowered his left foot and straightened, keeping in the shadow of his horse. His hand had dropped automatically to his gun and his cold eyes were hard and alert.

"Shore must be important," Tranter growled. "Look at 'im swing that quirt!"

Dorne, as he watched the oncoming rider, felt a vague prickling along his scalp. It was a feeling his system had reserved for times of danger and unusual stress. It told him this man would be the bearer of disquieting news at best.

As the buckaroo drew ever nearer, Dorne could see that he was stretched low above his horse's neck, where he could and was with quirt and spur exacting the best his wiry mustang could give. The fellow's hat, by the wind of his passage, was plastered back against his head; only its thin strap held it on at that breakneck pace. The horse's nostrils were wide and blowing, and of a sudden there was a perceptible falter in its stride.

"That's a—Hell!" Dorne swore, stepping into view of the coming horsemen, "that's one of the boys from the ranch! Now what? Ain't there no dang end to the trouble that jumps a sheriff's way?"

"Cripes, no!" Tranter muttered. "Sheriffs an' their depities is jest nacherly targets fer trouble an' ring-tailed rannyhan's pistols!" And he snorted, adding: "It's a livin' wonder to me we ain't been blowed plumb off'n the map a'ready!"

"Before you got so ancient a prune looked young beside yuh," Dorne growled, "I bet yore Maw called yuh Sunshine!"

"You know it! I was the sunniest jasper—"

The rest of Tranter's brag was lost in the crash of the oncoming horse. The rider shot forward over its head and lit on braking bootheels; came to a sudden slithering stop before the officers. Dust, ballooning up from around the threshing horse, almost obscured them. Through it, the rider barked:

"Listen Bill! There's sheep all over our range. Thousands of the blattin' stinkers! Range boss said tuh git the word to yuh quick if I had tuh bust a gut tuh do it!"

"Sheep!" Tranter snarled. "Sheep in a cowman's country?"

"A whole damn lan'scape filled with 'em!" the puncher croaked. "Bah-h-h! Bah-h-h! Cripes, it's enough tuh makes the ghosts o' cowmen turn plumb over in their graves!"

Up to this point Dorne had said nothing; he did not say very much now, but it was potent: "Borst!" The single word connoted many possibilities. This, that word told Tranter, was Borst's revenge!

He opened his mouth to speak, but Dorne beat him to it. "Who'd you put in charge of that round-up posse? An' have they left?"

"They've left!" Tranter said emphatically. "Half an hour ago. An' that Bar B Smith from Sunset County's got charge of the posse. I figgered he'd make 'em look harder bein' some of his own critters was mixed in, too."

Dorne nodded, and the tiny move saved his life so close had the shot whose echoes now beat back and forth between the buildings missed him. So quick were his reflexes that his own gun was out and spitting lead toward the window across the street, where a flash had marked the sniper, almost as the lead whistled past his ear.

"Round up another posse an' hold 'em here! I'm goin' to get that lousy son—but I'll be right back!" Dorne snapped, and went plunging through the hock deep dust toward the Black Bottle Bar, from one of whose front windows the bushwhacker had let loose his murderous slug.

Even as Dorne went crouching forward in a zig-zag run, the fellow fired again. But his nerves were jittery now, evidently, for the shot went wild, and through its dimming echoes Dorne could hear the pound of scuttling hoofs.

He reached the steps of Ortega's joint and cleared them in one bound that carried him smashing through the batwing doors in time to see Fisk darting through the gasping crowd toward the door of a back room.

As men jumped right and left to get out of danger Dorne drove three swift shots into the door Fisk's outstretched hand was reaching for. Fisk froze with blanching cheeks and shoved shaking hands above his head, one of which still held the smoking pistol with which he'd tried to snuff Bill's life.

"You damn shoot-an'-run killer!" Dorne's voice snapped savagely across the stunned silence. "I'd ought to gut-shoot you as a moral lesson to the rest of yore yeller breed! Drop that gun."

Fisk dropped it without parley. His twitching

lips and shaking hands told the terror he was in. He was trying to stammer out some framed-up explanation but the words did not make sense.

Bill crossed the floor in swift strides. He got one hand on the collar of Fisk's shirt and shook him like a terrier. Fisk's eyes seemed popping from his head when Bill desisted and snarled, "Where's the money Fuddabaugh an' Smoky Leupp took outa the Stockman's Bank, you dirty crook?"

"It's—it's—it's still in there," Fisk stuttered, trying to get his breath. "They never took it out—I just transferred it to my own private safe. But I was forced into it," he pleaded. "Borst made me a party to that—"

"Made hell!" Bill swore. "If you had a backbone 'stead of a wishbone, you'd 'a' had the guts to tell Borst where to go! *You're* goin' to jail—*c'mon!*"

They reached the street without untoward incident; in fact, without any demonstration of any sort on the part of the crowd in Ortega's dive.

There was a brightness to Bill Dorne's eyes that warned them he meant business, and his savage stride said plain as words that he had his war paint on and was ready to take on all comers!

"How'd Harniss' knife come to be in yore vault?" Bill asked, as he shoved Fisk into a cell beside Ortega. "Thought Harniss was workin' with you an Borst?"

"I told you before I ain't got no connection with Borst," Fisk said desperately. "He forced me into this deal. Said he'd have the bank looted anyhow, an' that I might's well help him out an' take a cut. If I wouldn't agree, he was goin' to have them gunmen rob it anyway, an' shoot me so's I couldn't talk!"

"Oh, yeah?" Bill said sceptically. "Well, what about Harniss' knife?"

"That was Borst's idea of a joke. He had Mendota borrow it an' then gave it to me to plant."

"Nice playful fella, that Borst," Bill commented. "But I gotta kinda hunch his playin' days is about wound up. You're goin' to be in here now anywhere from ten days till a month before yore trial comes up. You'll have time to ponder on the error in yore ways. I'll have Gospel Jones lend you a Bible so's you can see what the Lord thinks of yore kind of skunk."

Slamming the door on the now-spluttering Fisk, Bill sprinted for the front of the Sheriff's Office where he found that Tranter had raked up a second posse in record time. Six men, counting the ragged deputy, sat their saddles with Savage repeaters across their knees; six men with stern, determined faces—solid citizens who were tired of the sporting element's lawless rule. Bill sized them up at a single glance, and knew they were men to ride the river with, sturdy warriors who could be relied on.

He outlined the situation relative to the sheep he suspected Borst of bringing into the country, and did so in a few choice words. Then, climbing into the saddle, he said:

"Do yore shootin' first an' yore talkin' afterwards. Let's go!"

Globe's frantic eyes were fixed upon the open door. Whirling in his chair, the Wineglass manager saw that a man was framed there against the starry night. A man in the black frock coat, rusty string tie and flat-crowned hat of a gambler—a man with blazing killer eyes above a jeering twisted mouth that drawled with wicked softness:

"Fella—keep yore seat. My business is with that yaller-striped polecat, Globe."

Globe's face was ghastly. His lips were working, but no words came forth.

Tumbleweed laughed across the tightened silence. "Been quite a spell since we seen each other across a room, eh Frank?"

Globe whispered, "Trull! My Gawd—*Trull!*"

"Guess you been figurin' I was goin' to stay in that damn jail for life, eh, Frank? Guess you didn't hear I'd busted out. Well, I did an' here I am. Been a long wait, Frank, but this is sure worth it," and he laughed again, a chilling, mirthless cluck of sound that sent a shiver over Globe and caused him to take a few uncertain, backward steps.

"No, Frank," Tumbleweed went on in that same soft wicked drawl, "I ain't in the pen now, an' I ain't dead, though that last is what you're goin' to be right sudden. You've taken a look at yore cards an' we're ready for the draw. Frank," he grinned, "I'm goin' to put you under the daisy roots—down there with the rest of the worms where you belong!"

And even as he finished speaking a jet of flame licked out from his hip.

Globe was reaching for his gun when Tumbleweed's lead struck him, whirled him half around and crashed him sideways where he struggled desperately to maintain his feet. But failed.

He was done and Tumbleweed's pistol had not even cleared leather. Nor did it clear leather now as he backed slowly away from the door into the night from which he came. But his pistol's snout stared wickedly at the Wineglass manager from the open toe of its holster. And the ranch manager made no move for he rightly read the look in Tumbleweed's shallow eyes.

Marcia Globe sat motionless in the chair where the departing Lola had left her. No tears coursed down her cheeks from which all colour had fled. And her deep brown eyes were dull with pain and in her lap her hands twisted nervously at a fold in her gingham dress. How long she had been sitting there she did not know. But suddenly a step on the porch roused her, and the slow glance she sent in that direction told her that it was dark and that the stars winked coldly against the distant skyline. The figure of a man was outlined against it too, a darker shadow in the darkness of the open doorway.

She did not know who he was and could not make out his features, but the unmoving, unspeaking presence of a man staring at her as he must be staring made her catch her breath. And a faint tinge of fear came into her as she realized that this house was at the edge of town and that she was alone with this unknown watcher.

Softly, slowly, that he might not observe her movement—or if he did, might not guess its significance—she reached for the matches in the little tray beside the lamp on the nearby table. When she found them, she turned sidewise in her chair and with her left hand raised the lamp's chimney as her right hand struck a match and ignited the wick. Nothing happened as she replaced the chimney and turned the wick to the proper angle. Swiftly, then, she flashed a look toward the door.

The man still stood there—a Mexican in range clothes, and he was smiling with a gleam of teeth.

"'Allo, Keed," he said, and widened his grin for her approval. One arm was extended across the doorway, its hand resting on the opposite side of the frame from which his pantherish body leaned. With the other hand he was caressing a tiny black moustache. "Feelin' lonesome?"

"What do you want here?" Marcia said and got to her feet.

"You, señorita; you," Mendota said with a leer that drove her backward behind the doubtful safety of the table. "I'm theenk thees is w'at you call the beeg night for Pedro Mendota, no? The whole damn town, she seem to be away on vacation; only the sporting crowd here. An' they," he added suggestively as he advanced into the room with a catlike grace of movement, "weel not care what happens weeth you."

Dorne and his hard-riding possemen, attracted by the swift flashes of gunfire and the sharp flat reports of rifles, veered southward once they struck Bill's Picketwire spread, and headed for that part of his range adjoining Globe's. A battle was in progress over there and they were anxious to get into it and wind things up in a hurry, so as to leave them free to drive off or exterminate the hated sheep.

"Supposin' it ain't Borst that's back of this sheep business?" one of the posse called.

"It is," Bill growled. "It's got all the earmarks of his kind of deal."

"That's right," put in another man. "There ain't nothin' too raw for Pecos Borst. An' he's been layin' fer you, Bill! He ain't aimin' to lose his Hashknife spread if he can rely on it. An' rubbin' you out or crowdin' a passle of woollies onto yore range may give him a chance to dig in an' get set to grab his ol' place back again."

"Sure," Tranter put in. "With Bill outa the way there wouldn't be no Sheriff's sale of the Hashknife property. He knows that well as we do. There ain't no one else in this country got the guts to face Borst down the way Bill's been doin'."

"Looks like my boys have got them fellas holed up in that pile of rocks over by Big Toe Butte," Bill grunted to Tranter. "D'you suppose Borst's with these sheep? Don't hardly look like he would be."

"Naw," Tranter snorted. "He'll be in town, knowin' you'll be out here fightin' off them dang blattin' ba-ba's he wished on you."

"Gosh!" Bill ejaculated suddenly. "We plumb forgot about Tumbleweed an' Globe. Buck, you take charge of this posse—I'm goin' to the Wineglass, pronto!"

Lather was coming out along the edges of Bill's saddle blanket like shaving soap when he slid off his heaving bronc before the Wineglass ranch house door. That something was wrong he'd known as soon as he'd topped the ridge, for Globe was not in the habit of having lamps lit in every room—not all at the same time, leastways. So now he was out of the saddle and across the porch before his winded horse had slithered to a stiff legged stop. The next instant he was hammering on the door.

"Hetton!" he called to the manager. "Open up! It's me, Bill Dorne!" And—"Where's Globe?" he asked when Hetton, pale of countenance, stood in the abruptly opened door. "Anything wrong?" he added mechanically, although he knew darned well something was off colour besides the manager's complexion.

"Globe," Hetton said in a hushed and solemn voice, "is dead, Bill—murdered in cold blood not half an hour ago." Briefly, then, he gave Dorne the story. Dorne took it hard.

"I had a hunch somethin' like this was goin' to happen. I was headin' out here to warn Frank, when one of my punchers came larrupin' into town with news that some damn skunk has driven a flock of woollies onto my best range. If I'd only come on here directly—"

"You'd have been too late then just the same," Hetton said. "I blame myself for not doin' somethin'. Hell, I was sittin' right there when the whole thing happened." He flushed. "I can't understand why I didn't try to stop that son—but if you'd 'a' seen his damn eyes—"

"I've seen 'em before," Bill growled, "an' I'm hopin' to see 'em again right soon! I'll see you later," he muttered, and swung toward his horse.

"Hell, you can't ride that nag any place—not for some while, anyhow," Hetton protested. "Wait a sec. I'll have one of the boys rope you out a fresh one."

While this was being done, the Wineglass manager said, "What was that you was oratin' about sheep?"

"There's sheep on my range, driven there, I don't doubt, by Borst," Bill answered. "An' they're driftin' towards Wineglass territory now. My boys an' a posse I brought from town are out there foggin' up the birds that brung 'em. I figure Borst is prob'ly in town now, fixin' some trap for me or somethin'. What's more, I'm goin' to give him a chance to spring it. I'm headin' for town right now. I got a hunch that most of his crew—what ain't with the sheep—are in town with him. Tumbleweed's likely headed there, too. Probably Borst's figurin' to take the town over again an' get set while I'm tendin' to those sheep."

"Hell," protested Hetton, "you can't fight Borst an' the sportin' element by yourself, man! They'll—"

"Well," Dorne answered grimly, as the Wineglass puncher came up with a fresh mount, "I'm figurin' to."

And while the Wineglass manager was still protesting about the foolhardiness of such a course, Wild Bill Dorne swung one hand to the horn and slapped his left foot into the stirrup. The borrowed bronc was moving at a hard run when Bill settled into the saddle.

XXIII / "HUNT UP GOSPEL JONES"

As Mendota advanced upon the table, Marcia had to summon all her will-power to resist the urge to back away. But some inner voice told her if she left the doubtful sanctuary of this insensate bit of wood, all would be swiftly irrevocably lost. She was not sure of what it was she was afraid, but there was a tiger gleam in Mendota's dark little eyes she found distinctly sinister.

Mendota chuckled, catlike, a little purr of sound that roughed up gooseflesh along the girl's spine. But she would not give way to hysteria, she told herself. She would be brave and courageous and face this thing out. She came of pioneering ancestors, hardy stock whose courage in the face of adversity and threatened danger was beyond question—like Caesar's wife, as Tranter would have said. But Tranter was not here now to help her, and Bill—No, she mustn't think of Bill in this hour of need. For Bill had failed her shamefully. Outwardly Bill was all fire and fine-tempered steel, but inwardly he was like the spongy core of a rotten apple; a philanderer, a despicable Lothario who preyed on young and innocent girls, and led astray even wiser ones like Lola. No, Bill was out; she would not see him again. Or if see him she must, it should be a brief and icily courteous meeting wherein her only words must be negative.

It was strange, she told herself, that she could think these things at a time like this, while that Mexican was slowly closing the scant interval between them. It was as though she were detached and aloof from herself, as though this tableau was being enacted by other people and she was observing it from a safe distance. But she wasn't; it was she this swarthy renegade was stalking.

For a moment, as some tipsy reveller's footsteps went past outside, his striking profile was toward her as he listened. Then with a shrug he swung his shoulders toward her and there was a bold intentness in his eyes and a cynical salacious curve to his thin, cruel lips.

She caught her breath as he reached out and grasped the table's edge in one strong brown hand. Fascinated, she watched the swelling of the muscles of his bare arms and the cord-like strain observable in his long fingers. It came to her that he was about to hurl this fragile shelter aside and leave her without protection from this thing he had in mind. She tried to scream, but no sound left the parchedness of her mouth.

Through the wind-whipped night, Bill Dorne rode low along his mustang's neck with the hard-running animal's mane slapping his face, and his cold hard eyes keenly alert for any sign of ambush. He rode well away from brush and chaparral wherever possible, for he knew how tempting were such shadowy spots to killers of the type employed by Pecos Borst.

His fury against Borst and Ten Spot Trull burned like a white flame in his mind, excluding all other thoughts; excluding even thoughts of Marcia Globe, save as he was vaguely aware of the hurt and loss which must be hers when news should reach her of her father's murder. Her foster-father's murder, that was—for Tumbleweed, alias Ten Spot Trull, was her real father. It was a fact he did not intend allowing her to ever learn. For such knowledge could bring her no happiness. No, the past's secrets were better buried in the past.

His antagonism toward Borst was like a mighty river, an accumulation of minor angers and resentments, commingled with the bitterness of public wrongs and personal prides. Even before election to the shrieval chair, Dorne had not cottoned to the big boss of Spavined Nag; and since election he was determined to rid the town of its incubus. Straight from the shoulder he had made this plain to Borst, and Borst's doings and schemings since that date had been his manner of defiance. But this foisting of sheep on a cowman's paradise had been Borst's crowning insult—Borst's final throw.

Dorne was sure he'd find the man in town, and he was likewise certain that most of Borst's big guns would be there with him, awaiting Dorne's arrival for the final scene. That Borst would have the cards all stacked was a lead-pipe cinch. But true to his name, Wild Bill Dorne cared not a damn. He would smash Pecos Borst though all hell, hot lead and high water stood in his way.

For these last few miles Bill had been riding with a loose rein, letting his gallant mount pick its own way pretty much. But now, nearing town—indeed, seeing the twinkle of its distant lamps—Dorne crouched low in the saddle and applied both quirt and spur. If the fates decreed that by some foul chance Borst should go free, Bill Dorne would go down fighting after the manner of his kind.

Pedro Mendota's lithe brown arms were around Marcia fiercely, and his hot laboured breath was against her face. One shoulder of her gingham dress was ripped and fallen to expose the white creamy flesh beneath, and Mendota's lewd and avid gaze was on this intently as they struggled back and forth above the wreck of the broken table. Marcia's silent battle for her virtue and perhaps her very life was no more silent than was Mendota's stuggle to overcome her resistance—to "gentle her" he would have said—for when it came to a thing he coveted, Pedro Mendota was a man of few words.

Only the laboured panting of their breathing, and the stamp of their shifting feet, made sound in the narrow room. And to them, had they been less intent on their own hopes and fears, the tinpan music and oaths and laughter of Spavined Nag at play would have come faintly through the open door and windows. But they heard nothing, not even the soft clump of spurless boots, until—

"A bear with the women, ain't you?" a rough voice drawled with wicked softness.

Over his shoulder as Mendota tensed Marcia saw the ugly, seamed and jeering leathery countenance of the man leaning indolently in the doorway, even as Mendota himself had leaned not so many minutes before. There was a long and livid knife-scar on that countenance, that running from chin to ear along the left side. And the eyes below the stranger's hatbrim were pale, intent and sinister.

Mendota flung loose of Marcia's form and whirled on squeaking bootheels, handicapped by the lust and blind red rage that gripped him, and by surprise at this interruption to his desires. Yet even so, his spinning leap was like that of some startled cat, and just as fast and sudden.

Marcia, standing paralyzed with fear three feet away, heard the rip of steel on leather as Mendota's racing palm smacked gun-butt; caught his snarled *"You damn' peestol-tipper!"* Then the room was shaken by a rocking, roaring world of jarring sound, and it seemed as though her eardrums must surely be shattered.

She saw that flame appeared to burst from the

region of both men's thighs simultaneously. Yet it was Mendota's wiry form that seemed to suddenly lean as though to meet the spurt of flame that belched from the ugly stranger's bottomless holster. Then the hinges of Mendota's knees were letting go and he was crumpling, sagging forward on the old worn carpet.

And when she looked at the doorway the man with the ugly scar was gone, fading into the black night as silently as he appeared. And then she knew no more until she opened her eyes to find her head pillowed in the lap of the faro-dealer, Lola, and heard Lola's husky voice making soothing sounds.

"I lied, *querida*," Lola was whispering softly. "Oh, God, can you forgive me for such lies? I lied when I said those things to you about myself and Wild Bill Dorne . . . I said those things because I knew it was you that Bill was crazy about an' was going to marry. And I wanted him myself—you'll never know how much I want him, need him! I loved him the first time he came into Pecos Borst's Golden Stack Saloon. There has been a terrible hunger in my heart for a man like Bill; I've always dreamed of being loved by such a man and when I saw Bill I wanted him, and I made up my mind I was going to have him. But I can't go through with it, Marcia Globe—I can't! I thought I could, and I've schemed and killed and lied to get Bill Dorne. But he won't have me—it's you he wants, so I'm telling you those things I said were lies."

Marcia was gazing at her with new life in the brightness of her deep brown eyes; new life and hope—incredulous hope.

Somehow they found themselves upon their feet, facing each other, and Lola was backing toward the door. For the first time she saw Mendota's huddled body, and she screamed and thrust one hand across her mouth.

"My Gawd! What's happened here?" she cried, her eyes growing green and narrow like a startled cat's. "Who killed that breed?"

And Marcia described mechanically the things she'd noticed about the ugly stranger, and Lola gasped, *"Tumbleweed!"* and ran for the door.

In the Black Bottle Bar Lola found Pecos Borst, and a flame flared up in his smoke-grey eyes when he saw her and a low chuckle boomed in his bull-thick throat. "The prodigal returns to the fold," he sneered, and started toward her.

But she seemed not to notice the rash grin that tightened the bold line of Borst's thick lips. "That Tumbleweed killer of yours has run amuck!" she cried insistently. "Mendota's layin' dead on the Mayor's carpet—"

"Yeah," Borst purred, "and what were you doin' at the Mayor's house?"

"I was—" Lola began, and checked herself, and

the creamy whiteness of her unrouged cheeks went a pasty grey as she realized she could not admit to Borst that she'd been angling to get Bill Dorne. And yet, the thought struck her suddenly, she might do worse than tell a part truth which could be twisted to her advantage. "I was over there laying pipe to trap Bill Dorne—"

But Borst cut her off with a savage laugh and caught her by the shoulders in his big rough hands. "You damn little liar!" he snarled, his florid face going livid as he thought that here again Bill Dorne had beaten him, stealing from him this girl's love without even visible effort. "You've been layin' pipe to add Bill Dorne to yore conquests, you little slut!"

She tried to raise her arms to slide them around Borst's neck but he held her paralyzed by his rough grip, and she saw the passion and resentment in him mounting like a wall of water. Abruptly he released her with an oath, a shove from one hamlike hand sending her crashing back against the bar, and she saw the grins on the faces of his watching men. Something seemed to snap within her and her right hand sought the neckline of her low-cut gown.

But it never touched the tiny pistol nestled between her breasts. Borst knew of the gun she kept there and he guessed what she was about to do. Flame darted from his hip and smashed her back against the bar; again and again he fired as though to ease his mighty spleen, and when his gun was empty, she lay in a silent, huddled heap across the rail.

Bill Dorne slid from his lathered bronc before the hitch rail fronting Ortega's resort with the crash of gunfire in his ears. He did not pause but, yanking his gun, ducked under the tie-pole and took the dive's board steps three at a time and burst his sudden way through the swinging doors.

He saw the lifeless body of Lola lying there across the brass footrail of the bar. And he saw Borst with the smoking pistol still in hand, and the wooden-faced gunslammers that ringed him, clawed hands poised above their holsters. Phoenix John, Dode Harniss, Krayson, Gleed. And he saw Borst's narrowed eyes whip toward him and slowly widen, proving Borst had not been expecting him so soon.

"Woman-killin' added to yore line now, eh?" Dorne said bitterly. "You damned low-down rotter, Borst—you'd oughta be boiled in lard. Yes, an' by cripes, I'd admire the job of stirrin' you round in the kettle!"

"Always the blusterin' big bad bull in the china-shop, ain't you, Dorne?" Borst sneered, transferring his gun to the left hand, thereby telling the watching sheriff that it was empty. "Hell, I don't need to use a gun on yore kind of fourflusher," Borst added, with a sneer, and threw the weapon across the room—drawing another from beneath his coat as, momentarily, Dorne's eyes instinctively followed the thrown gun's parabolas.

But Dorne saw Borst's second movement out of the corners of his eyes; saw too the reaching hands of Borst's gunslammers darting thighward, and his own pistol came up in a burst of flame as the room appeared to sway and buckle with the monstrous detonations. Then, through the powder smoke, he saw Borst doubling up, clutching wildly at his middle, lurching backward. And he saw Dode Harniss fall slantways across a poker table, and Gleed scuttling for a window. Lead was tugging at Dorne's neckerchief, at his vest; he felt the jar of impact as a slug tore the heel from his right boot. But still he crouched there, wreathed in a fog of gun smoke, his forty-five jetting streaks of flame as he drove hot slugs across the ten-foot interval.

And then suddenly it was over, and the crash of guns but dimming echoes. Krayson was backed against a wall with his hands stretched high and empty above his head, his bronzed features gone a pasty, mottled white. Harniss was an outstretched motionless entity near the far end of the bar, and across Lola's motionless legs Pecos Borst lay sprawled, and something about his posture told Bill Dorne that the boss of Spavined Nag was boss no more—would never rise again.

Half an hour later, having locked Krayson in a cell alongside Ortega and Banker Fisk to await a trial that seemed assured of being marked by the stamp of Justice, Bill Dorne went into the Sheriff's Office and slumped heavily in his chair. He was sick of fighting, weary of the sight of blood and crooks and violence. He wanted peace and Marcia Globe and—but he had to wait for the reports of his two posses. He got them, too, several hours later, when close to dawn one of the men who had gone with Bar B Smith to recover the stolen cattle, rode in to report that his own and Smith's and Globe's had been located and were being driven to their respective ranges by the posse.

Ten minutes later, Tranter rode in and dismounted stiffly before the hitch rail. He stamped grumbling into the office and growled at Bill:

"Some night! But by cripes, we drove them lousy woolies to hell-an'-gone back onto Borst's spread an' into his fenced north section. Shot up four-five of the herders that was with 'em. An' say! Yuh know that bouncer, Gleed, what used tuh work fer Borst? Well, I come acrosst him ridin' his bronc like mad. Looked like he was headin' fer the Mex border. I hailed 'im but he kept goin' like Lucifer was headin' him with a pitchfork! I reckon he's goin' yet—if his nag ain't give plumb out!"

Bill told him tersely of the fight in town.

"Well, I'm shore pow'ful sorry I wa'n't around tuh lend a hand," Tranter said dolefully. "I guess this about cleans up this hell-roarin' range. Reckon bad men'll be at a premium after the county pays off fer the ones that's been snuffed in the las' few hours. Hey!" he added hastily as Bill got up and started for the door. "Where'n heck are you goin' *now?*"

"I'm goin'," Bill said grimly, "to hunt up Gospel Jones before any more trouble pokes its head over the horizon to delay again my already postponed noopshals. I'm goin' to get married—that's where I'm goin'! Marcia's waited long enough, an she's goin' to need a man's sympathy when she learns that her ol' man was murdered out to the ranch last night. I'm figgerin' on gettin' hitched up soon's I can locate that psalm-singin' sky-pilot. *Got any objections?*"

"Hell, no!" Tranter said, grinning. "Them's the best words I've heard yuh say since I come tuh Spavined Nag!"

Center Point Publishing
600 Brooks Road • PO Box 1
Thorndike ME 04986-0001 USA

(207) 568-3717

US & Canada:
1 800 929-9108
www.centerpointlargeprint.com